Reason and Romance

TERRANCE LAYHEW

Reason and Romance
© 2022 Terrance Layhew

Print ISBN: 978-1-66782-772-8
eBook ISBN: 978-1-66782-773-5

CHAPTER 1

Autumn

No party of any kind is absent agenda. Every person who walks through the door has one. The agenda may be grand or petty, innocent or malicious, but it is always there. Guests know who they do or do not wish to speak with, where they want to sit, and the outcome they hope for from the occasion. Few look at it so clinically, or ruthlessly, but even the most gracious of guests has a reason that propelled them from the comfort of their own home to someone else's. Even if it is as simple as a free meal.

Samantha stood by the door, watching and greeting the dinner party guests as they arrived. She surveyed the room to ensure they were appropriately engaged and comfortable. She knew her brother's agenda for the evening; hers was to see it accomplished. George had remarked she would make a great event planner, and she didn't doubt it. While in grad school, the twenty-four-year-old had moved into her brother's home and became the majordomo. She made sure his life moved with minimal friction or inconvenience.

"Mr. Newcastle!" she greeted the guest of honor. "So happy you could come tonight."

"If I'm dragged back here for a wedding, you can't imagine I wouldn't visit my favorite author, do you?" he said with a smile.

With the magical summons made, George Austen, author of six New York Times best sellers, appeared like the genie from the lamp. "Henry, great to see you!"

The friends shook hands, and George led him away to the study. Both men knew why they were there and saw no reason to wait to conduct the business at hand.

"Samantha!" Helen Newcastle greeted the hostess upon appearing on the threshold.

"Helen," Samantha said, mustering a smile. "So glad you could make it."

"I'm sure." Helen smirked. "I've invited a friend of mine to come along tonight, if that's alright. Normally I wouldn't, but she's a good addition."

Without missing a beat, Samantha replied, "There's an extra setting at the table. I like to be prepared, just in case."

"George and Daddy are already talking business?" Helen ventured.

"They have a half hour to hide away," Samantha confirmed. "That was as long as George said he needed, so that's what is on the schedule."

Nodding, Helen surrendered her coat and began to mingle. Samantha didn't know the daughter of George's editor well, but well enough. Willowy, with dark hair cut at shoulder length and coal-black eyes, Helen Newcastle was striking, but cold as ice. As she was about to ponder Helen's agenda for the night, Samantha's phone vibrated with a text message. Glancing at the screen, she smiled. Before the next guest could enter, she hastily sent a reply that she hoped would result in a smile on the other end.

In the study, Henry Newcastle sat across from George. Each held a small glass of whiskey with three ice cubes slowly melting into the amber alcohol. Whereas the rest of the house was neat and organized, George had made no effort to tidy his workspace.

"I see you have kept your sister away from here," his guest observed, looking around at the papers scattered and open books balanced on every flat surface.

"Samantha's greatest talent is knowing where to stop," George agreed, taking a small sip as he reclined in his chair.

"I hope the... disorder," the editor said tactfully, "implies there's progress on the new book?"

"Where you see chaos, there is an order," George defended himself. "Order that I alone may be aware of, but still exists. You only suffer from want of being me."

"As we all do, I'm sure," Henry said with a dry laugh.

"The book is almost finished," George assured him. "I'm adding the final touches to the last chapters, some minor details to give it polish, then I'll turn it over to your abattoir for the slicing."

"I'd hardly compare a publisher to a butcher's shop. Our aprons aren't even stained with ink, let alone blood."

"I was thinking more of the editing office, but I see your point."

"What about the next one?" Henry asked, taking another sip. "That's why we're in here while you have face time with me, right?"

George smiled. The two men got along not just because of a shared history—Henry had mentored George in his early career—but because they each knew how to cut to a matter. "I'm not sure yet," he admitted, "but I will be beginning it as soon as I turn in this one."

"Any ideas?"

He shrugged. "Nothing in particular. I expect to have the idea by the time of writing, at least."

"And this is supposed to comfort your editor instead of your agent?"

"My agent is already having epileptic fits. He's just glad I'm waiting until this one is finished first before trying to sell the next one."

"But you're still talking to your editor about it?" Henry asked with a sly smile. "What do you want to hear from me?"

George smiled back. "The same as any other author does. You adore my writing and are going to be interested in wherever my thoughts take me."

"There's nothing to worry about," Henry said, waving his hand. "We've been very pleased with your work and are excited to see what you write next." He paused to finish his whiskey. "Now we've discussed work, what about you? Where's your life these days?"

"On a steady upward trajectory," Helen Newcastle said, letting herself into the study without ceremony.

"Helen," George said, "glad you could make it tonight."

"I'm sure you are," Helen agreed, sarcastically. A flash in her dark eyes.

Henry laughed, allowing his glass to be refilled with a finger of whiskey.

Helen took in the room around her. It was much as she would have expected. Her eyes glanced across the shelves, the messy desk and side tables, hesitating a moment in their survey when they caught the title of a certain book lying dejectedly in the corner. Yes, very little about the room surprised her.

"If you're casing the room for valuables, I keep the rare editions under lock and key," George cautioned.

In response, Helen only smiled and said, "Your sister sent me to say your time is up, and I couldn't agree more."

It was a full table—the mark of a successful dinner party, George decided. He was seated at the head of the table, with Henry and his daughter to either side of him, while Samantha took the foot. Next to Helen was seated a young woman he was unacquainted with—not entirely shocking, but he thought he knew everyone on the guest list. He might not have noticed her at all, if she wasn't the perfect contrast to Helen. The latter was raven haired, with dark eyes and skin as pale as ivory. The woman beside her had auburn hair, almost flaxen (if you knew what flax really looked like), and large brown doe eyes that took in everything. If Helen could be considered cold to look at, this girl had a warmth that you could almost feel radiating from her. It was a good description, George thought, and filed it away. In fact, he decided to use it to describe the murdered woman at the end of his book.

At the other end of the table, he saw Samantha holding her own court. Talking animatedly about something, holding everyone enraptured. They were hanging on her every word, and exploded with laughter once she hit her punch line.

As the company around her giggled, Samantha checked her phone again.

It did not take long for the conversation around George to drift toward literary things. Henry was pondering trends in cover designs when Helen broke into the conversation. "What did you think of *Good Intentions*, George? I know Daddy sent you a copy to review."

"Romance is a worthless genre," George stated without hesitation. "I threw it into the corner the moment I opened it," he added casually, waving his hand in the air for emphasis.

"I couldn't help but notice it lying in the corner of the study," Helen commented. "Did you at least read any of it?"

"Why would I? Romance novels are not written for serious thinkers. They appeal primarily to the unsatisfied and lovelorn. For those who look for a fantasy to substitute reality and are desperate to feel for a moment, even if it's only on the page."

"Couldn't that be said of all fiction, that it appeals to those who wish to escape from their reality?" asked the young woman seated beside Helen.

"Perhaps in a broad sense," George conceded. "Romantic fiction, however, preys particularly on the intellectually weak and emotionally vulnerable."

"You didn't read it at all?" Helen asked again with feigned surprise.

"Only the dust jacket. After which, it was flung into the corner," George said unapologetically.

"It has sold very well," Henry interjected hastily. "A top seller with great reviews."

"I think it only proves my point about the hopeless state of the majority of readers in the world," the author scoffed.

"Perhaps when your next book is published you'll be so lucky as to find an audience lacking in literary taste," the young woman said.

"I'm sorry," Helen said, a malicious smile crossing her features, "I haven't introduced the two of you. George Austen, meet Ms. Margaret Clarke, author of *Good Intentions*."

Now George saw it, the jaws of the trap closing in that smile. "Congratulations at the success of your book, Ms. Clarke. I'm sure it's well deserved," he said. As sincere as he was, George sounded condescending, but he didn't care. He wasn't there to congratulate or coddle.

"I accept your congratulations," Margaret said graciously, "but I am sorry to discover you have such a narrow view of literature."

"Literature is broad, but my distaste for your genre of choice is personal," George tried to deflect, his interest tired of this topic and ready for the next one.

"You belittled everyone who has ever opened a romance novel. Ascribing to each an inability to find love or affection beyond the pages of a book. Do you enjoy *Ivanhoe* by Scott, or maybe *Lorna*

Doone? These are romances. Even *The Three Musketeers* is a romance in the true sense. When you write off an entire genre, you are discounting the best simply because you dislike the worst."

Helen didn't bother to hide her grin. George repressed his scowl, and surprise.

When dinner was eaten, most of the guests began to leave. It didn't take long for only the core of the gathering to remain: Henry Newcastle's party and the Austen family. It was here George intended on reasserting his control over the conversation, which he expected wouldn't be too hard. He opened his mouth to begin a lecture on something he found fascinating and naturally assumed everyone else would also. But before he could speak, Helen Newcastle did.

"Samantha, why are you blushing so?"

"Well," Samantha said, her cheeks flushed with slight embarrassment, "Margaret's practically a female Sherlock Holmes."

"It's really nothing," Margaret insisted. "I simply made a few observations that Samantha didn't expect."

"You can't leave us there," Mrs. Austen declared. "What did you say to cause Samantha to turn as pink as a poppy?"

"She said she knew there was a man in my life, recently added," Samantha admitted.

The news surprised George, but apparently not his mother. "That's remarkable!" Mrs. Austen said. "How did you know?"

"It's really nothing," Margaret said with a laugh. "A parlor trick at best. The amount of times she would look at her phone, and the expression she would have when reading or sending a message, suggested a romantic connection recently developed."

"Since we are in the closest thing to a parlor for miles around," Henry said with a chuckle, "perhaps we could induce you to repeat the trick for the rest of us."

"Since I happen to know something of how this works," Helen interjected, "I know it requires the observation of someone's appearance and actions. Could you give as accurate a read on someone who has a manufactured persona?"

Margaret considered a moment before replying, "I can only observe what is there to be seen, but no matter how much effort we take in managing our appearances, there is usually something about ourselves left to see."

"George is a man who takes care with how he dresses and presents himself. What can you see about him?" Helen prompted.

"Oh yes," Mrs. Austen encouraged her, "what about George can you learn by looking at him?"

George felt Margaret's eyes fix on him and rake across every inch, from the bottom to the top. He kept his expression neutral; there was little point in doing anything else. She appeared to evaluate him from every angle, her eyes shifting almost imperceptibly. George knew this form of observation was possible. He also knew just as well it was a trick employed by charlatans and mediums throughout history. Yet, she had been able to notice something about Samantha even he didn't know.

Her findings finished, Margaret closed her eyes a brief second and let out a breath. "He is studied in his appearance," she reported, "but attempts to do it in a way that appears natural, making up for this with an aggressive ease in the company of others. Mr. Austen makes it a habit of forgetting meals when working on a literary project. He is more athletic than he lets you believe. Life for him is a problem to solve, not an experience to live. When in the company of others"—she paused a moment—"he uses a veneer of sociability to prevent people from thinking him cold and heartless, though he knows it doesn't always work."

The room fell silent. Henry, Samantha, and Mrs. Austen all stared at George. Even Helen Newcastle watched him, waiting for a reaction. His face was hardened; his teacup hovered midair halfway between his mouth and the end table beside him. Quickly, he recovered. He replaced the cup on the table, resumed his nonchalance, and gave a wry smile. "Impressive," he said, "although, usually *I'm* the one warned not to trust first impressions. Henry, I came across a book I wanted your thoughts on."

Without any further discussion, the topic of conversation was redirected and no one ventured to bring it back to where it started.

After everyone had left for the night, George was sprawled on the couch. Head reclined, eyes fixed on the ceiling above him, eyebrows knit together in consideration. He thought a cigarette would suit the moment, but the prospect of lung cancer weighed stronger than the image of coolness he might capture for an instant. The whiskey was good though, two fingers of Jack Daniel's Sinatra Select over three ice cubes. The cool liquid warmed his mouth as he took a sip.

"Whiskey post–party." Samantha observed, taking a seat across from him. "It was a good night for all of us." It wasn't unusual for her to find her brother like this after a party; in fact, it had become something of a tradition. George would be taxed after a large social gathering, and as he recovered from his "social hangover" they would postmortem the night's activities. There wasn't a chance in hell she was going to miss this one if she was paid to. With a cup of hot tea in one hand and a bag of microwave popcorn in the other, she was settled in for the entertainment.

"Margaret Clarke is... morbidly fascinating," George pronounced, declaring it like a king pronouncing life or death.

"'Morbidly fascinating,'" Samantha mused. "How every woman longs to be described."

He silently ignored her.

"She read you like a book. How did that make you feel?" she asked with a little too much enthusiasm. Who could blame her? So used to command, to being unflustered, her brother rarely appeared anything less than perfectly put together.

"Like I should probably read her book." George sighed. He explained how he had unknowingly belittled Margaret's work and readership. "Knowing she was there wouldn't change my opinions, but I might have been a little less harsh."

When there was no response, George peered over to find she was intently texting. "Have you heard a word I said?"

Samantha held up a finger. Finishing her text, she returned her attention to George.

"That was him, wasn't it?" he asked irritably.

She ignored the question. "You acted condescending to a new author about a genre you avoid like the plague. Somehow you think you'd have acted differently if you had known you were talking to the author of the book," she summarized, popping a kernel in her mouth. "I think you would have said the exact same thing, maybe with more humor, but she's smart enough to have heard the exact same thing."

He knew she was right, even if he didn't want to admit it aloud. He took another sip of the Sinatra. He wasn't unfamiliar with putting his foot in his mouth; it happened. People usually forgave words uttered in haste sooner than he would regret saying them.

Margaret's assessment of him rankled, but was bearable. He'd heard it said the truth was often more bitter than lies, and this might be one of those cases. Helen, the manipulative wench, had engineered the encounter, luring him into speaking about *Good Intentions*. She had been the one to direct Margaret's assessment too. He considered what his best options for retaliation might be. A few ideas presented themselves, but none that could be immediately taken. Best to take his licks now and wait for time to present the best opportunity for revenge in the future.

"She's pretty, you know," Samantha observed, breaking her brother's reverie.

"Who?"

"Margaret Clarke," she replied dryly. "Her eyes are rather fetching," she teased.

"Yes, she is," George agreed matter-of-factly. "As many women are. And if you expect me to say more on the matter, you have less wit than I credited you with."

Samantha laughed. "I'm not unrealistic," she argued, "but I'm still hopeful to see my brother live happily ever after."

"That! That is the problem!" George declared, rising from his reclined position on the couch. "Why is it the only 'happily ever after' comes with love, romance, wife, and the like? Is it not conceivable to anyone a man could live contentedly without these things, spending his time as he likes, living the way he chooses and never venturing to the altar?"

"On a different note," Samantha said, changing the subject from one she had no interest in hearing about, "what's the beef between you and Helen anyway?"

George sighed and swirled the ice in his whiskey. "Who knows," he replied. "She's jealous of my success, she thinks she's competing for her father's affections, she's a sadist who delights in the pain of others... Take your pick. It could be anything, or nothing. Neither of us can probably remember or care."

It wasn't a satisfactory answer for the younger sister, but it was the only one she was going to get.

The Austen siblings were not the only ones who reviewed the dinner party later that night. Helen and Margaret discussed the company's conversation and activities at length. Helen praised the concise appraisal of George Austen that Margaret had made, enjoying the discomfort it must have occasioned her jousting opponent.

This didn't matter to Margaret, whose ears were still stinging from the tactless way George had "written off" her writing. Writing that came from hours of deliberate work and mattered to her as all words matter to a writer of care.

"It was ungenerous of him to say," she declared.

"He is not known for being anything less than he is," Helen observed knowingly.

"Hardly an excuse," Margaret fumed, ignoring for the moment how the entire conversation had been prompted by her friend. "A calloused heart," she decided. "He's like a vampire who lives off the blood of his victims."

"I think there's a far less colorful explanation," Helen corrected, remembering a past best left to the past.

"I prefer the vampire story, it's more dramatic."

The two young women giggled, leaving George to his judgements—obviously incorrect ones, given the warm reception *Good Intentions* had enjoyed universally.

CHAPTER 2

When the ceremony ends, the real occasion begins. At the reception, George took his place with the rest of the wedding party. His eyes darted around the room, looking over faces both familiar and new. Anthony and Katherine were glowing, their expressions beaming their joy and happiness. It wouldn't last, George reflected. Emotions never did. Somehow, people thought themselves the exceptions to the natural law of entropy. Everything ends, and feelings manage to do it quicker than most. Books, on the other hand—they endured longer than even the most ardent feelings anyone could ever possess.

Among the members of the audience he recognized were Samantha and the Newcastle party. Margaret Clarke had joined them, apparently. If Katherine and Helen knew each other from college, it stood to reason she knew Margaret also. Where was his mother? Gazing around the room, he found her seated next to a young woman near his own age, talking with a broad smile. She caught his gaze and waved him over. He shook his head. She waved again; he shook his head again. Finally, she and the young woman came to him. Not the result he had intended.

"George," Mrs. Austen said, "this is Kelly Masters, a friend of Katherine's from college."

"Hello," George said, restraining the mortification growing inside.

"Hello," Kelly replied with a laugh.

"She's a big fan of your books," Mrs. Austen explained. "I said you were always happy to talk with your fans, especially the cute ones."

George smiled and tried not to commit matricide with his glare. "I'm happy to talk with any fan," he corrected, then turned back to Kelly. "Which book did you enjoy most?"

"I think it was the one with the tower," she decided.

"Ah, yes, *Born in Babylon*. One of my earlier books. What about it attracted you?"

Kelly pondered. "I think it was the female protagonist."

Born in Babylon didn't have a female protagonist. George needed an escape, as this conversation was not going anywhere he wanted to follow. "Watch this," he said, lifting his champagne glass and tapping it with his dinner knife. The sound echoed throughout the room as more people joined in, forcing the newly married couple to kiss. After the cheers had finished, George rose and excused himself to Kelly, saying, "Always great to meet a fan. Be sure to be on the lookout for my next book, to be published soon." Retreating to the bar, he ordered a gin and tonic and toasted his masterful handling of the situation. She might even buy his next book, even if she never read it.

George's relief was short lived. Out of the corner of his eye he could see his mother approaching again with another "fan." This time she didn't even try to warn him in advance. Ignoring her, he dropped a fiver on the bar and walked into the obscurity of the crowd.

Safety was discovered in a small chapel off the lobby to the reception hall. Deciding an unlocked door was permission enough, George let himself in. It was not a large room, but perfectly adequate for his needs at the moment. Drink in hand, he relaxed on a padded pew near the small lectern at the front of the room. The stained glass window behind it depicted familiar imagery: the cross and an empty tomb. "Original," George muttered, taking another swig of the gin and tonic. Removing the notebook from his breast pocket, he scratched out a note about stained glass. It could be a powerful image to use in his next book, providing it captured something poignant and possessing.

Hearing the chapel door creak open, George stiffened. He hadn't anticipated either being found this quickly or his mother being so aggressive. Surely he could be permitted a fraction of peace and quiet. He didn't move a muscle; like a child caught in the cookie jar, he hoped an absence of movement would prevent his detection. The door widened and a woman in a pale yellow dress crept inside, a look of relief on her fine features.

"I can leave," George said, rising from his seat, "even if I was here first."

Margaret Clarke jumped. "What are you doing here?"

"Hiding. The better question is, what are *you* doing here?"

She crossed her arms. "Just because I'm nicer than you doesn't mean I don't get tired of being around people too," she said, but added, "You don't have to go if you don't want to." She flopped, delicately, on the pew opposite George.

Resuming his seat, George took another sip and sighed.

They sat in silence. He didn't have anything he could immediately think to say, and the quiet was nice. He didn't expect it to last long, but it did. Maybe she was expecting an apology, but he had already given the closest thing to one she'd hear at the dinner party the other night. She seemed to be content taking her time. When her eyes drifted his direction, he realized she was reading him again, just like she had the other night.

"A picture would last longer," he said with a smirk.

This seemed to draw her out from whatever evaluation she was making. A laugh dropped a second after she had time to think of it. "Good to be the one saying that for a change?" She teased.

"If you think I ever waste my time leering, you are a worse judge of character than I thought," he said, a cold note chilling the sentence.

"If you take that remark personally, you're softer than I thought," she countered with a half smile. "Did you get tired of your mother herding women your direction?" she asked with a chuckle.

"She's not the most subtle woman in the world," George agreed, rubbing his temples.

"But that wouldn't matter, you believe you'd notice even if she was," Margaret observed.

"Reading me again, Ms. Clarke?"

"Speculating, for the most part," she admitted. "You don't need to read people to know if someone believes themselves to be smarter than everyone else, they tend to exhibit it openly."

"And some people do it nicer than others?"

"Yes," she said, smiling. "*You* usually don't. In fact, Helen was telling me you believe yourself to be the smartest man in the room, and to make matters worse, you usually are."

"I'm shocked she was capable of complimenting me so directly."

"She's as committed to realism as you are. Said something about how it is better to deal with an unpleasant truth than a comfortable lie."

George took another drink. "She borrowed that from one of my books."

"You borrowed it from a book too," Margaret observed. "Nothing anyone really writes is original. It's just a retooling of another story from another story. As a matter of fact, there were a few very handsome young men out there with some wild stories about the famous author they know... Can you imagine they mentioned the connection the moment they heard I was a writer?"

"A man trying to form a connection with a woman based on the slightest of acquaintance? Shocking, really."

"Really," she agreed. "One of the groomsmen, I think his name was Tommy—"

"Bobby."

"—was telling me about how you kept them busy with this wild tale before the wedding. From what he described, it sounded an awful lot like the legend of the Hound of Ulster."

"Good catch," he admitted. "Anthony wanted me to tell them a story, I used the Irish legend as a template."

"I've always been partial to Greek myths myself."

"They tend to be overplayed," George said with a shrug. "Using an unfamiliar story gives me more liberty than aping Ulysses."

Margaret said nothing, instead returning to studying his expression. George did his best to return the favor. Try as he might, there was little he could attempt to learn from analyzing her features. She was, as he had assessed the other night, a beautiful young woman with wide eyes that would trap you in their depths. Beyond this, he couldn't discern anything about her character or actions. Observation was not why he became a writer.

"Why are you hiding?" she finally asked.

"You know why," he answered. "To avoid having my mother constantly shove adoring fans in my direction."

"That's the reason you gave, but I doubt it's the whole story. I know from firsthand experience you don't mind ruffling a few feathers if you can do it politely."

George almost winced. Instead, he stood up, walked to the stained glass window. Tilting his glass, the melting ice cubes began to settle.

"You write for 'why,' don't you?" he asked.

"Sorry?" Margaret asked in confusion. "I'm afraid you've lost me."

"I haven't read your book, but I'm pretty certain you write to answer 'why.' My theory is all writers write to answer a question of 'who,' 'what,' 'when,' 'where,' or 'why.' For example, I write to explore a 'what,' to use characters to expose and play with a theme. You must look to answer 'why.' Why a person would do this, or why they wouldn't. Motivation. 'Why' pushes people to do the things that books are made of."

"It's a pretty theory, but it also simply sounds like good character development," she observed.

"Mark my words, any book will be driven by a 'why,' 'what,' 'when,' or 'where,'" George insisted.

"Why then"—she paused to smile—"do you focus on 'what'?"

"'What's' the point," he said smugly, taking another small sip of his drink.

"Clever, but you should explain," Margaret replied, raising an eyebrow. She may have found him calculating, arrogant, and unbearable, but the role of professor seemed to suit him. She could see the answer to her question already. Sharing an idea animated him. It brought electricity to his ocean eyes and seemed to open up the real George, the George who didn't care about being as studied, as when she first cast her gaze over him. This was a man who could almost be considered likable, even without trying.

"In nonfiction we see ideas explained in detail, but fictional narratives offer a chance to show an idea lived out," he clarified. "We can see how the choice to do this or that. The 'why' you are attracted to is decided by a 'what,' a guiding theme that carries through the story and can offer the reader an insight into something they may have overlooked or ignored in their own lives."

"It has nothing to do with being more comfortable with ideas than people?" she prodded.

George only shrugged and shifted his drink again. The ice cubes had almost entirely melted, diluting whatever alcohol remained in the tumbler. He briefly pondered whether he should risk escaping for another, or…

He sat down in the pew in front of her. Lazily he grinned and asked, "Care for a drink?"

"I'd love champagne, actually."

"Fantastic, could you get me a gin and tonic also?"

Margaret laughed aloud; of course this was his play. "You're really so scared of your mother bringing you another fan, you're asking me to fetch you a drink?"

"I'm buying," he offered, extending a fifty dollar bill between his index fingers.

She swiped the money. "When I get back, you're going to have to give me a preview of your new book. Because I actually am a fan." She rose, smoothed her pale yellow dress, and left.

The way to the bar was crowded, but Margaret could see another benefit to her getting the drinks. When you're an attractive woman, the bartender tends to prioritize your interests. It was a form of discrimination she was happy to support. She glanced around the room to see what everyone else was doing. Morbidly, she was most curious to catch sight of Mrs. Austen's activities. Eventually she found the woman talking to Samantha and the Newcastles. Helen looked a little bored, probably wondering where Margaret had gotten off to.

She was tempted to drop her friend a text, but the idea of telling her later about her time with the vampire was too delicious to pass up. She'd wait to share the story, and it would be improved by Helen's curiosity at her disappearance.

Champagne in one hand, gin and tonic in the other, Margaret returned to the chapel. She opened the door as quietly as she had before and stole inside without attracting any attention. It was a little difficult with two full drinks, but she managed it with the dexterity of an experienced lush.

"There was a long line at the bar, but there are benefits to wearing bright colors and smiling," she announced. "You should try it some..." Her words tapered away as she looked around for George. She was alone in the chapel.

At first she waited. Perhaps he went to relieve himself, or was called away at the last moment for a groomsmen errand. Maybe they needed to decorate the getaway car for Anthony and Katherine. Margaret waited for twenty minutes before deciding to wait no more. Whatever good will she had momentarily possessed for George Austen was gone; he had proven himself to be just as calloused and inconsiderate as her better judgement knew. "Damn him," she muttered, shotgunning her champagne and leaving the gin and tonic sweating on the lectern.

It was only a moment after Margaret closed the door that George's mind began to snipe at him. What was he doing? This woman was dangerous: attractive, clever, and canny enough to see through his carefully crafted persona. The other night she had torn away at him and could easily do so again. Their conversation had been pleasant, but perhaps too pleasant? His warning signals were flashing, telling him to get out now while he still had a chance, before things went too far.

A part of him said he was overreacting. There was nothing to worry about here; Margaret Clarke did not seem to have any of the icy malice that Helen Newcastle could exhibit effortlessly. Maybe that was the trap? To lure George in with her warmth and apparently nice demeanor, only to pull the rug out from under him? Her retaliation might be with kindness assumed until it could cause him maximal harm.

Not everyone thought like he did, and yet… Was it worth taking the risk? What was the worst that would happen if he left now and found security amongst the groomsmen? He owed Margaret nothing; he had even paid for the drinks himself, he rationalized. There was more to lose if he stayed than if he left. He set his jaw and narrowed his eyes. The decision was made.

Any thoughts of Margaret closed with the door behind George. If he wasn't willing to let his family or friends entrap him, there was no reason he should lay a snare for himself. It was easy to slip back into the group of groomsmen. Anthony was still shell shocked and didn't even seem to notice George had gone missing at all. George asked Bobby to get him a gin and tonic from the bar and whatever he wanted for himself.

After leaving the chapel in anger, Margaret rejoined the Newcastles. Helen shot her an inquisitive glance, but mercifully didn't ask any questions. Samantha and Mrs. Austen passed by to pay their respects. "It was delightful to have you all over for dinner," Samantha said.

"The pleasure was all mine," Henry replied graciously. "The wedding today was beautiful, don't you agree?"

"Yes," Mrs. Austen said. "Almost perfect, but I was a little surprised not to see Cynthia here."

Unconsciously, Margaret noticed how Samantha's eyes flashed and the immediate discomfort that fell on everyone except Mrs. Austen.

"Yes, well, we should be going," Samantha said, hurrying her mother away with whispers Margaret couldn't hear.

Reclining in the uncomfortable chair provided by the venue, George observed weddings were occasions judged successful by virtue of the day itself, not the long-term results of the event. The success or failure of the marriage itself couldn't be judged by today. It couldn't even be judged by the character of the two getting married. He had known Anthony for years, and over that time he had changed; presumably, so had Katherine. The two people who got married today were not the same people who would celebrate their fortieth wedding anniversary. It was those people and the people they were in between who would make or break their marriage.

As honest an observation it was, George didn't share it aloud. At happy occasions clouded with emotion, very few wanted to hear a rational voice speaking with distance and impartiality. His role today was to support bride and groom and wish them the best, no more, no less. As time went on, he would hopefully be involved in their lives enough to remind them of the commitment they made today that would bind those future versions of themselves to one another. It was a part of marriage that made George wary—enslaving his future to a choice made in the present, a choice made with the blinding colors of emotions and feelings instead of logic or sound reasoning.

Internally, he heard a voice asking whether leaving the chapel was based on an impulse of emotion, but George ignored it. He had made the decision that offered a low risk and a high reward, and he would have been foolish to do otherwise. He didn't catch any sight of Margaret Clarke the rest of the night—by choice or by chance, he didn't know, and frankly, he didn't care.

CHAPTER 3

"Has hell frozen over?" Samantha asked with shock and amusement.

George raised his gaze over the book in his hands, drawn out of the story world by his sister's exclamation. Eyes rolled at her, then dove back beneath the pages.

After the wedding, and a long night's sleep, the first thing George did when walking into his study was to scoop up *Good Intentions* from the corner it occupied. Flipping the pages, he dropped into his armchair and began to read. Initially he only intended on reading the first two chapters, but when Samantha interrupted him he came to find it was already well past noon and he was well past the midpoint. Closing the book for the moment, he decided it was time for coffee. The manuscript for *Lord Wilmore* was submitted already, and he could spend the rest of the afternoon reading if he wanted.

A short walk down the road and over the hill later, he was at his favorite coffee shop. He excused the expense and effort visiting the shop required compared to making coffee at home by the walk. Writing was admittedly not a physically active profession, and getting those extra steps in got him that much closer to hitting his 10,000-step daily goal. George glanced at his watch. He was up

to 5,340 steps, so he could still hit 10,000 before the day was over...
maybe.

"How are you today?" the barista bubbled.

"Fantastic," George declared, placing his book on the counter.
"How about you, Cassandra?"

Cassandra smiled. "Great! On break from school. Pre-med has
been a killer."

"I'll bet. Favorite class so far?"

She thought a moment. "Probably physiology. What can I
get you?"

"Let's go with a decaf light roast if you've got it."

"Settling in with a good book?"

"Something like that," he admitted.

Chelsea looked at the title. "*Good Intentions* was so great! I
adored every page, the love story is so dramatic and heart wrenching.
What do you think?"

"I'm about halfway through. So far, I'm impressed with the
author."

"She's amazing. I can't wait to see what Margaret Clarke writes
next."

"Couldn't agree more."

Eventually, George had his coffee and eased into one of the
large easy chairs. Cracking the book to where he left off, he resumed
reading. It didn't seem long before the book was over and Cassandra
was gently clearing her throat and reminding him they were closing
in fifteen minutes. "All finished," he declared, drinking a final swig
of the now cold coffee.

Upon completing the book, his first reaction was to be satisfied in his assessment of Margaret's writing style. The book was indeed fueled and motivated by the 'why' of the characters. Well-written characters too, which made the story more believable considering it was drawn from an emotional core. For her first book it was remarkable. Even now, he avoided some of his first published books for his mental health. There were flaws, which could be in some ways excused because the story was sufficient to gloss over them. Yet, for all the warmth the book had, it didn't really seem to have any great depth. It didn't appeal to him as a thinking man. Instead, every word and effort appeared directed toward winning his heart. Entertaining, but not enlightening, he reasoned. It was a sentence eloquent enough to use in his review.

When George arrived home he settled into his office, laptop at the ready, to begin writing a review of *Good Intentions*. He glanced at his watch: only 7,047 steps. He knew he'd do some pacing. Probably not enough to make it to a full 10,000 today, but then again, he might. Taking a deep breath, he began to type.

Des Moines, Iowa is a quiet capital city. Low maintenance and as Midwestern as they come. Better compared to Madison, Wisconsin than Springfield, Illinois. What made it better than either of these, in Margaret Clarke's estimation, was the existence of a certain local coffee chain, *Smokey Row*. It was here in these booths she had pitched her novel to Helen Newcastle, outlined the story, and fell in love with her characters. Sentiment anchored in a physical location—she adored it.

"Did you read the review yet?" Helen asked without preamble as she slid into the seat across from her friend.

"Which review?" Margaret asked, eyes widening. Her iced mocha was sweating onto the table. Taking a napkin, she dabbed at the dew.

"By our vampire, Mr. George Austen," Helen answered, eyebrow cocked and smirking.

"The question is if he actually read it before he wrote it," Margaret spat bitterly. She hadn't told Helen about the incident at the wedding, the embarrassment of fetching him a drink only to have him disappear. Helen was one of her best friends, but Margaret knew her well enough to know that kind of ammunition would be stockpiled for future use, not allowed to rust away like she wanted.

"I think he definitely had to, to write this," Helen explained, tapping on her phone. "Just sent it to you."

Unlike most reading on the phone, Margaret didn't skim the review. She read every word carefully. Not that George's opinion really mattered, but he was a significant enough author that his words could potentially carry weight among other readers. Her face ran through various expressions as she read, a smile shifting into a frown and back again. Helen watched, waiting expectantly like a mouse fixated on a block of cheese.

When Margaret had finally finished the review, Helen waited a beat to drink from her coffee (taken black). "Well?" she asked, "what did you think?"

"'Entertaining but not enlightening, Ms. Clarke's debut novel is all it promises to be as a romance novel. Appealing the heart in every way but not offering the mind any arguments to persuade it,'" Margaret quoted irritably.

"Which he says along with a lot of good things," Helen observed. "George wouldn't offer any praise he didn't believe is deserving."

"Right, you two and your code of rational accuracy," Margaret replied with an eye roll.

Helen shrugged. "It keeps both of us honest. Wouldn't it be more terrifying if we weren't?"

"Because the two of you would somehow become more annoying?"

"More dangerous," Helen corrected. "Instead, we only use our claws on each other."

"Yet you're not using this to incite me against him?" Margaret probed.

"There's no value in trying to incite you against him," Helen defended. "I genuinely thought you'd be interested in seeing someone who disparaged your writing so vehemently could actually enjoy it once he gave it a read." She couldn't read expressions as accurately as her friend, but a shadow passing across Margaret's face wasn't hard to read. "Is there a reason you assume I'd use this to fluster you?" she asked.

"No," Margaret insisted. "I just know how you used me at dinner that night."

"If you expect me to apologize, you're going to be waiting. He didn't say anything he wouldn't have said at any other time. I just opened the door, he chose to walk through it."

Margaret sighed. "I didn't bring it up to argue or fight about, but I don't like being anyone's cat's paw. If you want to scratch out George's eyes use your own nails, or anyone else's, just not mine."

"Deal," Helen agreed, nodding.

They shook hands over it, the pact now solemnly decided and settled. Helen had suspicions there was more beneath the surface, as she knew her friend was far more capable of affection than she herself. George was an objectively handsome man; was it possible...? The data was just too inconclusive. She'd never quite understand how emotional beings operated in the world, but it was far more entertaining to watch them flounder than to try figuring out why they abandoned their good sense to start with. It was one of the things that made George a good opponent. They both understood the world as it was, not as they desired it to be. Where was the fun in manipulating the simple when the true challenge was in facing your match?

The two women enjoyed their coffee and managed to find time to gossip about more than George, but Margaret didn't forget about him. All the while, she was trying to decide what to do. Strategy was not her forte. Helen would probably have proposed a dozen different revenge opportunities within minutes. Margaret could always ask—it might even make Helen's day—but doing so after explicitly asking her to stay out of their games wasn't an option. Instead she let the idea fester. It followed her from Smokey Row to her gym, throughout her exercise routine, and eventually back to her apartment, where she was greeted by a small package waiting at her doorstep.

Nine times out of ten these packages were additions to her ever growing library. The passion she had had for books as a child never stopped; if she had the money and the book she wanted was there, she bought it without hesitation. The worst that could happen was she never actually read the book, but she always had the option to read it if she wanted.

It didn't take long for Margaret to tear into the package once her apartment door closed behind her with a clash. Casting aside the cardboard debris, she was left holding a book wrapped in brown paper and tied with a string. A note was placed between the top knots. She removed it and read, "The author asked to ensure you receive an advanced copy, since he heard you are a fan." Signed by Henry Newcastle. She cut the twine and removed the paper to find a copy of *Lord Wilmore* by George Austen. It was at that moment she knew what to do. It was deliciously appropriate, too. Immediately she texted Helen, "I'm going to write a review of George's new book, know anyone who will publish it?" Within a breath she had her reply. Tomorrow she'd read the book, the next day she'd write her review.

Just as she planned, Margaret read *Lord Wilmore* in a day. She returned to Smokey Row, tipped well, and smiled to ensure she had fresh coffee at her fingertips all day long (decaf substituting for regular around noon). She had read George's previous books and wasn't awed by his style, but now, having met him and learned what drove his story, she read it in a different way than she might have. There was a twofold respect, the first from having written and published her own book, and the second in the strength of his story and the insight it was trying to offer. *Lord Wilmore* did not threaten you with its ideas like a bully in an alley; instead it was willing to share, if you asked the right questions. It provoked her to ask those questions, just like when she and George talked in the chapel. The memory brought a flush to her cheeks. Tightening her jaw, she remembered her mission at hand. It was not to compliment, it was to critique. But where to start?

Unlike Helen and George, Margaret hadn't sworn an oath to rational accuracy, but she didn't want to lie. If she was to wound George in a review, she knew it would have to be an honest one—one that would point out the glaring flaw of both the book and the man. Fortunately, she had already had the opportunity of reading George himself. The words and the argument had already begun to formulate themselves, stacking word by word and sentence by sentence.

CHAPTER 4

I t had been a week since *Lord Wilmore* was released, and for the seventh day in a row, George found himself uncertain what to write about. This was the first time in five novels he didn't have a next project ready when he finished the previous one. At first it hadn't worried him. As when he talked with Henry Newcastle, he had shrugged it off, confident he'd know what to write when the time came to start on it. Yet, here he was… waiting for a muse to bless him with insight.

Anyone who isn't self employed imagines the schedule designed by those who are must involve sleeping late and working when needed, goofing off for hours on end, and doing just enough to justify being paid. While George didn't doubt there were some writers who lived life like a long weekend, he had never managed to live like that himself. Frankly, the inactivity would have killed him. He rose early to greet the day and had a schedule he maintained. Certain days were devoted to specific exercise or training of the mind or body, but each had a routine and a demand. George always showed up for work. As a writer, that work was different than day laboring, of course, or even office drudgery, but it was still work. He knew he had an enviable job, and he chose to remind himself of that when it became difficult and it didn't feel like writing so much as digging for words like a paleontologist searching for fossils.

Today was no different. There was a schedule to keep, and he could only plan to show up, even if the words and inspiration did not. After his workout at the gym and the first cup of coffee was poured, he settled behind his desk to complete his morning pages. Free-flow consciousness onto the page—he completed three of these a day, filling folders on his laptop in case the ramblings ever became useful. It was a practice that forced him to empty himself out, abandoning any shame or inhibition. Everything went onto the page. A sentence might start and lead nowhere, but just as often, it became a beautiful newborn sentence that grew into a paragraph and sometimes matured into an essay. Those births of ideas were rare, but when they happened it was the miracle of life.

At the present moment his morning pages contained lots of thoughts dropped into white space, few of them connecting to others. He hadn't come across anything that amped him for action, for pursuit of a story. George kept typing, even if it felt like it was going nowhere. "The process matters, the process would get him to his destination," he typed, hoping the words set into the pages would make it so. "So let it be written, so let it be done," he typed next.

The pages were finished, their contents devolving into various clever double entendres and modified curses. The idea of his future biographers coming across the endless composition amused him— the initial reaction of joy at so much material unearthed, and the rapid disappointment to find the quantity of useless rambling and eighth-grade humor to sift through.

George found himself in his local coffee shop again, enjoying his table. The pressures of writing left behind in his study. Samantha had begun to ask about his next project; apparently she was becoming concerned about his lack of productivity, even threatening to mention it to their mother. If he was hiding here, she couldn't very well know what he was doing with his time, now could she? When inspiration was scarce, he found some solace in reading. With *Good Intentions* as his last book read, he moved onto more meaty material in the form of a biography of Theodore Roosevelt—always the man to make you want to do more. George had to credit his success as a writer to the books he had accumulated in his mind over the years. The constant digestion of ideas from history and other authors, in connection with his life experiences, eventually spawned his book ideas.

"Someone's not writing."

George lowered the book to find Anthony Stapleton taking a seat beside him.

"It's called research," he defended himself, setting the book to the side and drinking his coffee. "All writers do it."

"But the difference is I know what it means when you're reading about Roosevelt. Is that the eighth book you've gotten about him, or just the eighth time I've seen you read that book?"

"Take your pick." George shrugged. "What are you doing here? I thought you were gone for your honeymoon until the twenty-first?"

"That was the plan. Don't think Katherine hasn't reminded me. Work called me back for an emergency."

"That's what you get working for three-letter government entities," George said with little sympathy.

"Eventually I'll transition to the private sector, or maybe I'll just become a writer like you."

"Then you'd never have a vacation."

"Anyway, did you see the latest review for *Lord Wilmore*?"

"It's taken five books, but I've learned to not obsessively read my own reviews."

Anthony took out his phone, saying, "I think you'll want to read this one." He pulled up the page and slid the device across the table.

"How's married life going, anyway?" George asked airily, his eyes only glancing at the phone, until his eyes caught the byline of the review.

"It's a little harder than I expected," Anthony admitted. "I'm imagining it must be different for couples that live together before getting married, but I'm just not used to having her there all the time."

George wasn't paying attention to anything his friend was saying. His complete attention was directed at the review, written by none other than Margaret Clarke. When he directed the publisher to send her an advance copy, he didn't anticipate her reviewing it; he actually hadn't even considered it a possibility. Now, he realized what a potential misstep that might have been.

George captured every word. It wasn't that he cared what she thought, of course, but the impact it could have on the casual reader was important. Finally he read aloud, "'George Austen's latest drama is a compelling mental exercise, designed to put the mind through its paces and challenge you to think, which is good because, much like the main character, it doesn't possess a heart.'"

"You're taking that out of context," Anthony observed. "She said a lot of glowing things about the book. You've taken the one negative remark."

"It was perfectly intended," George said, returning the phone after sending himself the link. "She wanted to try hurting me where she thinks I'm vulnerable."

"But she doesn't know you don't believe in vulnerability," Anthony replied sarcastically. "No, you're George Austen, ruler of all within your domain and rational to no point of fault."

"Are you finished?"

"Not quite," Anthony answered. "George Austen, the demigod here on earth who unlike Achilles has not even the exposed heel to harm."

"You've made your point."

"Have I? You can't make too much out of this. So what if your books are intellectual and don't possess the passion of heart. You make people want to cry sometimes, that's something to do with the emotions, right?"

George contemplated a moment. The muse had kissed him, bestowing her blessing on his next literary endeavor. He had his story. "Anthony," he announced, "I'm going to write a romance."

"That's a terrible idea!" Samantha said when George excitedly told her about his next project.

"That's what Anthony said," he replied, pouring himself a cup of hot tea. "And like I told him, I'll tell you, yes it's a challenge, but why not?"

"What happened to 'romance is a worthless genre'?"

"That is precisely why it needs me to redeem it with my literary skill."

"Whatever, it's *your* time," she decided, shaking her head in exasperation. "You're still planning on coming to dinner tonight to meet Charles, right?"

The truth was, George had forgotten completely about meeting Charles. He was apparently the beau Samantha had been hiding from him and his mother. Dinner was planned, first with Mrs. Austen, who gave her blessing to the relationship after learning he was the son of a cousin of an acquaintance ("Practically family!"), and now it was George's turn to meet the man who could ruin his entire domestic life.

Although he rarely considered it, Samantha leaving would interfere with his world more than he wanted. George had grown used to having her run his home efficiently and without comment. Her employment was certainly real and he could hire someone to take her place, but the little jokes and rapport between a brother and sister would never compare with the professional civility of any housekeeper he could hire. "Or you could get married," his mother had icily responded when he first expressed his concern. She was unsympathetic to say the least.

George arrived at the restaurant ten minutes ahead of the agreed meeting time—early enough to get his bearings and fortify his position. It also meant he could spend a little extra time reviewing the menu. Taking his seat, he assessed the room. Observational talent was not among his innate tool kit. He could look at things and know them through intuition, being simply the better guesser. But when he was about to start writing a novel, he needed to cast the characters. Find templates for personalities in the world he was populating. The names would come in time, but it started with simply who could he see in each part. Who would be the one to fall in love? There was a casting choice he hadn't made in the past. True, love had played a role in his second book, but it was so recently after... He chose to use it as the fulcrum of destruction for the protagonist. Now, he had to find a way to use it to bring life instead of death.

"Excuse me," a blonde woman about his own age asked, "are you George Austen, the author?"

"I am," he said, rising, "thank you for noticing. It's a pleasure to meet you..."

"Chelsea." She extended her hand.

"Chelsea," he repeated, giving it a shake.

"I'm a big fan of your work."

"That's very kind. Do you have a favorite book?"

"Well, I know it was just released, but *Lord Wilmore* was incredible."

"Authors never get tired of hearing such things," George said. "Would you like to take a seat for a moment? My party has yet to arrive."

Chelsea sat next to George. "The thing that really has me thinking, and I'm thrilled I get to ask you—is the old woman who leaves the flowers Wilmore's mother or not?"

"Good question. I left it ambiguous so people could make up their own minds. But," he added conspiratorially, "I like to think it's her myself."

"George!" Samantha called, rushing to her brother. He rose and gave her a hug. Beside her stood a man of medium height, a little younger than George and with dark hair, a beard, and bright eyes. "This is Charles," she introduced.

The two men shook hands. "I see you've already met my sister, Chelsea," Charles said.

George's head rocked to Chelsea, his fan, and immediately he felt betrayed. Trying not to show it, he smiled and resumed his seat.

"Hi Charles!" Chelsea said, giving her brother a hug. "When you said her brother was named George, and her last name was Austen, I didn't put it together until now."

Now George could see the familiarity between them, the same sparkle in their blue eyes. They almost glittered like gems, dancing in the light.

"An incredible coincidence," George said, and directed a discrete glare at his sister that she either quietly observed or ignored.

It did not take long after arriving home for George to pour himself a finger of whiskey. He looked at it, his glass filled just above the three lazy ice cubes. With a mental shrug, he raised it a second finger. He paced in the kitchen, a room that for the past two years he had spent little time within. Coffee, tea, whiskey, and vodka, sometimes water. These were the only reasons he really came to the kitchen anymore. George sipped on his whiskey again and loosened his necktie. Yes, he was annoyed, why shouldn't he be? Wasn't it enough his mother was continually trying to foist an unwanted addition into his life? Now his sister, on top of everything else, was beginning to do so also.

His thoughts were interrupted by the sound of the door unlocking. Whiskey in hand, he entered the living room and looked at Samantha and said nothing. His eyes, icy as the sea that swallowed the Titanic, communicated everything that was needed.

"Inviting Chelsea was not my idea," Samantha insisted, dropping her purse on the couch. "Charles thought it would be a good idea so you didn't feel awkward with the two of us."

"Great plan," George said sarcastically. "Nothing awkward in the slightest about meeting your sister's boyfriend for the first time alongside his single sister."

"It wasn't my idea," Samantha reiterated.

George dropped into his armchair and rubbed his temple with the sweating tumbler. "It wouldn't have been so bad if he didn't have to make a point of it. I was willing to endure dinner as pleasantly as possible, but did he have to say anything?"

"No," Samantha agreed, "he didn't, but don't you think Chelsea is even more embarrassed than you?"

"You have a point," he conceded reluctantly.

As a brother himself, George was still shocked with the turn of the evening's conversation. The four of them had taken their seats, George trying not to stare daggers at Samantha. Despite arriving early, he was the last to actually order his meal.

"I assume my sister was picking your brain about your writing when we interrupted," Charles said. "She's a big fan of your work."

"So she said," George agreed, concealing his annoyance.

"Did she convince you to spill the beans about your next book yet?"

"You and Samantha arrived before I had a chance," Chelsea said with a smile.

"Samantha claims to know, but has remained tight lipped about it," Charles commented.

"She signed a non-disclosure agreement," George explained. "If she says anything about it there are legal consequences."

Charles and Chelsea laughed.

"He's not kidding," Samantha said, drinking her water.

Charles and Chelsea stopped laughing.

"A writer takes his secrets seriously," George said, "which also means, as charming as your sister may be, I wouldn't have told her what my next book is about until I decided it should be common knowledge."

"That makes it easier to procrastinate on the next book, right?" Charles said, chuckling.

George didn't find the remark funny, and was about to say so, when Samantha cut him off, saying, "George likes to think of writing like a magic trick. The more you know how it works, the less impressed you are with it."

He might have said that at some point, George couldn't remember off the top of his head. It sounded like something he'd say, anyway.

"My charming sister is also recently single," Charles announced. "And I'm sure she'd be delighted to sign a non-disclosure agreement if you wanted to reveal more of your secrets to her."

There were only three times in his life George recalled being speechless. The first was when he received his first copy of his first novel. The second was when he found out he had insulted Margaret's book to her face. This was the third, and definitely worst, time.

The conversation was redirected by Samantha desperately observing something inane about the facial hair on one of the servers. Chelsea blanched, then flushed. Charles was oblivious. George said nothing; he couldn't. What could have been said to that?

"It's not that Chelsea isn't attractive," he explained to Samantha, reclined in his armchair, nursing the remains of his now diluted whiskey. "She may be a very nice young woman, but you know my scruples."

Samantha held her hand up. "You don't need to explain to anyone, let alone me. We've been through this. You're not looking for a relationship, and anyone who tries to force you into one might as well be the devil."

"You've been listening, great to know," George said with a smile.

George's view of Charles was currently tainted by what he viewed as a lack of discretion or tact. Rationally, he tried to remind himself everyone has moments where they seem to fall short of perfect character. Even he himself. Irrationally, he thought Charles was an impudent self-important prick.

The next day George retold the story to his mother when she came by for dinner. "Was she pretty?" Mrs. Austen asked.

"I think you've missed the point, Mother," George sighed.

"Not at all, you were mortified he would be so direct. Maybe he simply cares for his sister like your mother cares for you?"

"You don't need to make it worse," George said, shaking his head.

"Now's the time to take a break, focus on having a personal life for a change," Mrs. Austen decided. "You've become successful, why shouldn't you enjoy it, find someone to enjoy it with?"

George began to wonder if this was a secret plan devised by his mother to never receive another invitation to dinner from him again. He never thought Samantha's cooking was that bad. Instead of sharing this suspicion, he said, "Let's table this so I can tell you about my new book idea."

"Fine," Mrs. Austen agreed, settling herself in her chair. Ever since he was a boy she had been hearing his book ideas. Most of them never quite made it to paper, but it didn't stop her from encouraging him to give them a try. Even his worst idea was worth teasing onto the page. She was very proud of how he not only had become a published author, but hadn't let the acclaim go to his head. He had enough confidence for two people already.

Holding his hands together, George paused for a moment to collect his thoughts for the pitch. "I'm going to write a romance," he announced, spreading his arms and grinning.

"That's a terrible idea," Mrs. Austen said, mouth agape.

"That's what Anthony and Samantha said too."

"Perhaps there's a reason for that, dear."

"Of course there is, they haven't seen me do it yet."

Mrs. Austen pursed her lips. "I don't think that's the reason."

"How hard can love be to write about?" George asked. "It's just the same as any other story, but instead of a hero overcoming an external conflict with his enemy, he's overcoming an emotional one."

"You're thinking through something logically that isn't designed to have logic," his mother warned.

"People want love to be clear cut and defined," George argued. "It's impossible to find it like that in real life, so their needs are met by seeing it as clear in fiction."

"Do you have a story to tell yet? Do you know who you're writing about?"

"Mother, I've only just begun this process. The story hasn't had time to present itself. I only know it will be a romance."

"Don't commit to something you can't finish."

George rolled his eyes. "Fear not, mother dear, I won't breath a word of it even to my publisher until I'm certain it will work."

In the moment, he believed it would.

"What was wrong with your brother yesterday?"

Samantha sighed. George could be complicated to explain to someone who hadn't known him for long. Hell, he was complicated to explain to some of his closest friends. She and Charles were meeting for lunch and debriefing from dinner the night before.

"He's not fond of set-ups, suggestions of set-ups, or really anything that suggests romance in his life in any way or capacity."

"You'd have thought I was suggesting he bathe in a vat of acid," Charles complained. "It's not like I was trying to set him up with some acne-riddled third cousin. Chelsea's—well, you've met Chelsea."

Samantha sighed again. "It was partly the way you went about it. I'm guessing George thought it was a little hasty and presumptive." In fact, that was precisely what George thought, because he had used the words "hasty" and "presumptive" when he complained to her about it.

Charles slumped in his chair and hung his head back. They were eating outside at a deli and a small breeze began to pluck at the edge of his napkin. Before the next gust could take it airborne, he secured it beneath his plate. It was a small gesture, but it was in those few seconds he decided he wasn't going to give up on Samantha because of her brother. Visions of family Christmases and Thankgivings under his disapproving gaze danced through his mind. Never a sneer or ill word, just an iceberg of indifference. Charles was as human as the next man, and craved the approval of everyone he met. Perhaps it was a flaw, but he liked to be liked, and he decided he was going to win George over. After all, if Samantha liked him, why shouldn't George? Maybe it was just a matter of getting to know him better.

Reaching across the table, Charles took Samantha's hand in his and gazed into her eyes. "I won't take it personally," he said, giving the hand a squeeze.

"You shouldn't," she insisted, returning the gesture.

It was a rare moment when what Samantha said and thought diverged. George had certainly taken it personally, and it would take time for him to forgive the perceived insult.

CHAPTER 5

Winter

Among the perks of being an author were the speaking oppor-tunities. It actually made up a reasonable portion of George's income every year, allowed him exposure to promote his books, and, at the very worst, gave him a chance to travel at someone else's expense. He found he had a talent for standing up in front of a crowd and telling them about what he did and suggesting what they could do in turn. If he found the talent surprising, his mother and sister certainly did not.

It was with a smile he opened the invitation from the University of Iowa, located in Iowa City, to speak at a panel presenting on modern authors and their techniques. Iowa City had a healthy writ-ing community—though, granted, the last time he spoke at a work-shop there he wouldn't have classified anyone he met as "modern." It had been a room of elderly people who were filling in the free moments they had left. In that particular lecture, he focused on how they possessed something younger authors didn't: a lifetime of expe-rience to use for their material. It was one of the reasons he read as many books as he did. History supplemented what had yet to be experienced. Given this particular panel was for the university, he expected a slightly younger demographic.

"Are you going to try visiting the Newcastles while you're out there?" Samantha asked, attempting not to appear excited at her brother vacating for the weekend.

"Henry is out of town," George said, "and as you can imagine, I have little interest in seeing Helen."

"I don't know, it could be an opportunity for a surprise attack. Make a move on the board she wouldn't expect," she needled.

"Not worth the risk. I'll keep my distance from Des Moines and be back before you know it."

Which was precisely what Samantha was afraid of. "You don't need to rush back on my account," she protested. "Enjoy a change of scenery. Have an adventure."

"It's Iowa," George said flatly, "There's little to see and less to venture."

"You never know, something might present itself."

Subtlety was not one of Samantha's gifts. It was one of the reasons he was so surprised she had managed to keep Charles a secret for as long as she had. There was a reason she was trying to keep him away. George was about to ask a prying question when he stopped himself. It wouldn't profit him to push the matter. Better to watch events unfold. The times he tried forcing issues in the past had rarely played out well. Instead of winning a careful game of poker, he would likely find himself scrambling in a game of fifty-two-card pickup.

Iowa in winter is as pleasant as anywhere in the Midwest in winter, only more so. Roads are usually plowed, and people sometimes drive like they have experienced snow before. George was glad to get out of the car and into his hotel, happier still to escape the hotel and get to the college auditorium.

It was much like the other panels he had shared in. A long table set with microphones and a bored moderator ready to rein in the group. "Robert Smith, I'll be moderating today's discussion," he introduced himself. "Have you met the other panelists yet?"

George replied in the negative. Usually he paid attention to who else was involved, but this time he simply let it fall by the wayside. He had the topics and a general idea of the questions that the audience might ask. Speaking at an event like this, he actually found the less prior knowledge he had walking in, the more interested he was in participating.

"They should be arriving any moment," Robert continued, glancing at his watch, his voice a near monotone of disinterest.

"George Austen!" an unfamiliar voice declared.

Turning, George was confronted with a squat man with dark hair, beard, and complexion. "It is a pleasure to participate on this panel with you, my good man. Your books are revelations. *Lord Wilmore* may be the first classic written in our lifetime. The way you contrast the struggle for power and identity in the same arc, using politics as a mirror into the soul of man himself—"

"You are?" George asked, interrupting the unstinting praise the man was trying to bury him in.

Shock crossed the short man's face. "I thought you surely would have heard of me. I'm Paulo Castillo, a professor here at University of Iowa. I teach literature."

"Professor Castillo—"

"Please, call me Paulo," Paulo interrupted in turn. "I insist all my friends abandon such formalities."

George almost said it was a pleasure to meet the man, but he doubted it would be an honest assessment.

"I too am a writer," Paulo continued.

"Really?" George asked, tempted to observe that since it was the point of the panel which brought them there, he sincerely hoped so.

"Yes, but it remains unpublished at the moment."

George made no comment, but Paulo needed no encouragement. "Every time I think it is ready to be published, I find there's more to be written. More to be said. By the time it is ready, I think it will truly be the greatest American novel."

"Is that so?" George cast around for Robert's monotone voice and appearance to save him from this conversation.

"Truly," Paulo affirmed, apparently oblivious to his companion's disinterest.

George looked at the table on the dais again, where there were thankfully more than three microphones. The moment someone else showed up, he could leave them with Paulo and escape. He didn't have to wait long. A local mystery author arrived, whom George had already met at a previous function. Apparently Paulo was as unknown to him as he had been to George. After a brief introduction, George excused himself, citing natural functions. He felt a little bad; as he left he could see the mystery author's eyes widening with what Paulo probably mistook for awe.

George had ten minutes before the event began. After relieving himself, he ran the clock out by sitting on a bench in the lobby and people watching. Occasionally, when he saw someone interesting, he took out his commonplace book and made a note. If real life was stranger, or at least as interesting, as fiction, he might as well glean what he could. His phone chirped when it was time to get back to the panel—two minutes. He could simply walk in and take his seat and talk when needed.

The auditorium was fuller than he expected. A good sign for book sales, he thought. Which reminded him, had he brought his fountain pen for signing books? He didn't have long to ask himself the question, as quickly he was brought to reality by a voice he would not soon forget.

"George Austen!" Paulo declared, much as he had the first time.

"Paulo!" he replied in turn, taking his seat.

"I was excited to meet all of you," he explained, "but to meet in person someone so lovely was unexpected."

The conversation seemed to have taken a turn George did not expect, although, perhaps it could explain Paulo's apparent enthusiasm for his arrival.

"I appreciate the sentiment..." George began.

"Don't believe a word of it, the man doesn't believe in sentiment," a familiar woman's voice cut in.

Taking the seat next to George was Margaret Clarke, a playful smirk on her face. "His books prove the point," she added, her tone icy enough to frost Paulo's glasses.

"Margaret Clarke!" Paulo trumpeted. "I was just telling George how lovely you are in person to meet."

She blushed slightly, but accepted the compliment with grace.

"Ms. Clarke," George said with a nod.

"Mr. Austen," she replied as coolly. "Fancy running into you again."

"You two know each other?" Paulo asked excitedly. "Wonderful how such events as these can bring together old friends and introduce new ones."

The mystery writer took his seat, and Robert's monotone introduced the panel and their current works on the market. Most of the questions were general and as expected. They related to how they became writers and the routines they used to navigate what the event was marketing as "the write life."

George tried to remain engaged through the process. Margaret's presence was a wildcard he hadn't anticipated. Her review of his book hadn't faded from his memory; after all, it was the prompt which had him started (or at least preparing to start) on his romance novel.

The generic questions were asked and answered, the moderator nudging different members of the panel for their thoughts depending on the context or specificity of the question from the audience. In nearly each case Paulo felt the need to add his thoughts to the mix—certain, no doubt, of the importance of what he had to say. Of the four panelists, Margaret was the freshest author and the youngest in age. Her enthusiasm for the craft of writing and for sharing what she learned from writing her first book was contagious. Much like reading her book forced George to give her credit for her aptitude, seeing her today talk about the experience of writing forced him to be impressed with the attitude she approached the work with.

"How do you write a character who feels real?" an audience member asked.

The moderator passed the question to George first, who answered as succulently as he could. "Few of us want to read about real people. Instead, we want to be presented with heightened and better, or heightened and worse. Audiences don't want to read to feel like they are in real life."

"Can I add my thoughts?" Margaret piped in. Robert nodded and she continued, "Great characters start with the same emotions as real people. It means starting with driving wants and needs that will pull them through the story. If we can relate to their want or need, then they become real." Had she stopped there, George would have nodded and agreed, but she didn't. "For example, my co-panelist's book, *Lord Wilmore*, is a perfect example of a well-written, clever story whose characters are heightened, but at the cost of real humanity. We are made to think about these characters like they are angels or demons, not real people. Despite George Austen's talented skill, he didn't write real people, he wrote ideas and gave them names. Some writers are just better at appealing to the mind than the heart," she concluded with a smile at George, her eyes set with a sense of victory.

The eyes of the audience turned to George. Robert waited a heartbeat for the words to settle before he asked, "Mr. Austen, is there anything you'd like to say to that?"

He didn't rush to speak. George had learned early a dramatic pause and deliberate tone made for a more compelling way to not only convey your point, but make it more memorable. It was one thing to say he couldn't write a real character in a review, another thing to publicly question his competency as an author.

"From my perspective," Paulo leapt in, "readers are looking for a character that they can root for. Someone who they will hurt for when they lose and rejoice in their victory. They should be thinkers, but not at the expense of emotional heart. They should have heart, but not at the expense of having a mind. Why, in my book I'm writing—"

"My next book," George interrupted Paulo, "will be a romance." The words just dropped out of his mouth. It was a conscious decision made unconsciously. The cat was out of the bag. A slight murmur went through the audience. The one or two magazine writers he could recognize immediately went for their notepads. "Ms. Clarke is welcome to her opinion of how I construct characters. Personally, I think it is more compelling to appeal to a reader's mind, but I trust this next book will prove I am equally as capable of speaking to the heart as anyone."

"What can you tell us about it?" Robert asked. It didn't matter how disinterested he was; he knew enough to ask the obvious question.

"Nothing yet, just that it will be a romance."

"My book has romance in it," Paulo interjected. "Along with adventure and daring, the exploits of my protagonist are enough to rend the heart..."

The panel finished without further attacks from Margaret but with more descriptions of Paulo's yet unpublished book, and the fourth panelist probably walked away with the premise of his next murder mystery. George wouldn't have been surprised to see a character similar to Paulo meeting with a meat grinder.

Each of the writers took their positions behind tables near the entrance of the auditorium to sign copies of their books, inscribing them with special notes when asked. Not having a published book of his own to sign, Paulo hovered around the other authors, occasionally suggesting to a student they might like him to sign the book also. George assumed the ones who accepted the idea had to worry about him grading their papers. Years from now, they could look back on their signed first edition and shake their heads in wonder at the extra signature.

If anything, it appeared Margaret's comments only improved sales. Those who had already read *Lord Wilmore* praised it and tried prying for more details about his upcoming romance. In response he'd hold a finger to his lips and smile.

Finishing the signing, he was ready to leave when Margaret stopped him. "Wait," she said, "some of us are headed to a bar to grab dinner and drinks. You should join us."

Narrowing his eyes, George tried to decide whether he was still angry with her, and whether she was with him. He sighed. He had to eat sometime, and chances were she wouldn't try poisoning his food. "Sure."

"George Austen!" Paulo called, materializing beside Margaret. "I'm delighted you're joining us for dinner tonight."

There's the reason he had been invited, George decided. Margaret needed someone as interference between herself and the full force of Paulo's indescribable charm.

The place they found wasn't anything to note. It was a small bar that had a pianist playing jazz in the corner. Dinner was consumed without much conversation from George or Margaret, but Paulo didn't miss a beat. He kept up a steady pace of speaking with no one other than himself. His poor students, George thought, imagining what a class with him must feel like. When Paulo excused himself to the bathroom, a comfortable silence dropped between Margaret and George.

Seeing Paulo's empty plate, George remarked, "When was he quiet enough to eat?"

Margaret snickered, then resumed her composure. "How are Anthony and Katherine doing?" she asked.

"Anthony had to cut the honeymoon short because of work, Katherine hasn't left him yet, so I'd say it's going fine." Silence again, then he added, "I read your book."

"Did you? I almost didn't notice the review until Helen waved it under my nose." A note of bitterness in her voice, he judged, but not as bitter as before.

"I was impressed. It was mistake to cast it aside without a second thought," he admitted.

Margaret raised her glass. "Something we can both agree on." They toasted the agreement, unconsciously striking a truce at the same time.

"As to your review of *Lord Wilmore*..." he began.

She held up her hand. "Stop there. You don't want us to argue the virtue of heart or head, do you?"

"I suppose it's a little unproductive," he agreed.

"Especially when you're going to be joining my side," she teased. "A romance... What in the world prompted this?"

"First of all, my romance will appeal just as much to the mind as the heart. Second, none of your business."

Those dark eyes looked him over, reading him again. "My review really got to you, didn't it?" she decided with a laugh.

"That's your interpretation of events," he said with a shrug.

"There's no end to the senselessness!" Paulo proclaimed, resuming his seat. No context was given to his statement, and none was sought.

"Have you given thought to your next project yet?" George asked Margaret before Paulo had a chance to regain control of the conversation.

"Well," she began, "I have a few ideas, but nothing concrete yet. *Good Intentions* was popular enough, I could probably write a sequel and extend the story of the characters, but their story was wrapped up so well I'm not sure I want to do that."

"You could always continue the story of the supporting characters," George observed, "but you've probably already thought of that."

"I have. The trouble is I'm not really interested in seeing their stories continue. I'd rather find new people whose stories I want to watch unfold."

"You could write a YA novel," George teased. "Set it in a dystopian world, evil adults and a chosen one to save them all."

Margaret rolled her eyes. "That's too 2010s for my taste. I'd rather write about magic."

"In my book there's a magician," Paulo commented. "His powers may or may not be real. A challenge to the protagonist as he attempts to discover the difference between reality and fantasy. Ms. Clarke, I'd love to see how you would portray the magical world."

"Whatever you choose to write next, I'm sure it will be worth the read," George encouraged. He could remember the early days of his writing career, when it felt like his first book might be the only hit he'd write. It had been received with some acclaim; not so much that he didn't know he could do better, but enough to make him nervous about the viability of his next project. "You'll never know until it's finished," he said.

"Maybe I'll write about a lonely writer who finds people beneath his notice," she said with a hint of sarcasm.

"Seems a little far fetched," George replied. "If he finds people beneath his notice, he can't be all that lonely."

"It's the excuse he uses," she decided, her voice becoming serious. "It justifies why he feels alone. He tells himself they aren't worth the investment of his time or attention, but it's an excuse for why they don't invest in *him*."

Tightening his jaw for a moment, George's eyes became cool and frosted. "It sounds simple in a story, doesn't it? Reality is always more complicated."

"Sometimes it isn't."

"You try to read people, to break them down into understandable elements. You see a fact about a person, an observation, your extrapolation, but the narrative you create from it isn't guaranteed to be right. It is a fallacy to assume we can draw direct links from one event to another. Most of the time it is merely our nature telling us a story to give us the illusion of understanding in a world that is vastly more complex and random than we imagine. As authors we write stories that tell people how one event happens, leading to this or that happening after."

Paulo squirmed at the edge of butting in, but the look in George's eye dissuaded him from entering this arena. The conversation had risen above his weight class.

"It's always been my opinion if people begin to think they can guess what the story is like," George continued, "it's time to challenge expectations."

"Like leaving me holding your gin and tonic?" Margaret asked, her voice hardening.

Whatever kindness of God protects fools must have been watching over Paulo. He did the one thing George never expected from him: took a hint. "You two sound like you have a rousing discussion ahead of yourselves, but I should turn in. Teaching tomorrow!" he hurriedly explained, giving his goodbyes and leaving.

"Are you going to try telling me when you decided to walk away it was a choice based on rationality, on your stupid code of reason?" Margaret demanded as if there'd been no interruption, her voice rising.

George didn't answer. He knew when it was better to wait a beat before replying, so he took a sip of his drink and weighed the words he had to choose from. As an author, you always have to choose which words you will or will not use. There are dictionaries full of options to choose from, and thesauri full of variations, but finding the right word at the right time to properly express a thought or feeling is what the craft of writing is all about.

"You're angry?" he asked, buying himself more time.

"You have to ask?" she bit out, her displeasure clear as a grammatical error.

"I owed you nothing," he said, instantly regretting the words as he said them.

"You owed me the actions of a gentleman," she reproached him. "I actually thought you were going to be a nice guy for a moment."

"That was your mistake."

"You're telling me," Margaret muttered. The fury which she had held back began to push against her restraint, but how could she express what she felt to a man as unfeeling as a corpse?

"I chose to leave because I believed it was the best option," George explained unapologetically. "But I don't think I would have made the same choice today."

Now Margaret was quiet. Her eyes searched George's expression and demeanor. He wondered if she was looking for confirmation of what she thought, or if she was starting anew from scratch with what she could see.

"You're right, I look for 'why,' and you say 'what's' the point."

Silence fell between them. Heavy as lead, with neither accepting the burden of speech, only alternating between looking at each other and their drinks. It was George's experience that if you remained silent long enough, the person who last held the floor would speak again, but minutes ticked by and Margaret said nothing, made no move to leave, and indicated no frustration. She seemed content with things as they were.

He almost left himself. Once, twice, three times, George's mental voice warned him to leave now, to leave before anything could compromise him. Discretion, after all, was the better part of valor. But he didn't leave. He kept his seat, and they talked. Their truce now forged, the silence began to drift away like an early morning mist—a comment here, a giggle there. Comfortable camaraderie settled in as they shared about their favorite authors and what had first interested them in the craft of writing. They debated the merits of Dumas to Hugo, Dickens to Defoe, and countless other nuances which ink drinkers find fascinating to discuss. It was a breath of fresh air for George to speak with someone who could communicate as fluently about reading and writing as he himself. To the extent he could observe, it appeared Margaret was enjoying their conversation just as much, excitedly sharing how she had spent painstaking hours revising *Good Intentions* prior to publication. She compared catching the stray, unnecessary sentences in the manuscript to scooping a butterfly in a net.

"Did I tell you about Charles?" he asked, changing the topic of conversation, and related the story of how he was ambushed at dinner and the impudence of the man, both as a new acquaintance and as a brother.

"Was she pretty?" Margaret asked.

"Chelsea is an attractive woman," he admitted, "but that's not the point, as I apparently need to make clear to anyone I tell this story to. It's a matter of manners, and Charles has none."

"And he's dating your sister, and she likes him."

"There's the lay of the land."

Margaret thought about it a moment. "If you really don't like him, you could always try breaking them up."

There was an idea, and it wasn't an unattractive one. If he couldn't pull it off, could anyone? There was Samantha's heart to consider, but she was too infatuated to see the damage such an idiot would cause in the long term. That was the problem with feelings; they clouded better, sounder judgements. Charles had to go, it was as simple as that. "A brilliant idea," he decided.

"I wasn't entirely serious."

"I am."

"Well, if you need any help, you know who to call."

"I'm sure you'd be a great help, but…"

Margaret laughed. "I was referring to Helen, actually." Then she added, "But if you need help with your book at all, there I might be able to help."

Now George laughed. "Thanks for the offer, but despite what my family and friends may think, I know what I'm doing."

Taking a napkin from the bar, Margaret wrote out her phone number and handed it to him. "Just in case you're mistaken"—George started to interrupt, but she halted him—"which I am sure is never the case, here's my number. And although I don't have a book to never finish or a class to torture tomorrow morning, I do need to call it a night. But before I go, I need a favor." Reaching into her purse, she revealed a copy of *Lord Wilmore*. "Would you mind signing it for me?" she asked innocently.

George took the book and, opening to the flyleaf, signed it with a flourish, resisting the urge to add a witty or clever remark with his name. Instead, he asked, "Are you sure you didn't want Paulo to sign it too?"

She nearly fell off her seat with laughter.

They made their goodbyes and parted at the door. Risking a glance over his shoulder, George caught a sight of Margaret's retreating figure headed for her car. For all the absurdity Paulo had uttered that day, he was absolutely right in one respect. Margaret was a lovely sight to behold. Rationally speaking, of course.

CHAPTER 6

It was with purpose George returned home. He had his mission: to break up Charles and Samantha. He had his book idea: to prove he knew how to pull on the heartstrings as well as anyone. He even had Margaret's phone number, not that it mattered. He was home and, opening the door, he was horrified.

"What have you done?" George demanded, looking around to find nothing the way he had left it.

"Good to see you too," Samantha replied. "Yes, it was a wonderful couple of days while you were gone."

"What have you done?" he repeated, eyes darting from object to object in the living room, relocated from what he had always regarded as their proper place.

"While you were gone, I decided it was a good time to deep clean the condo and move a few things around."

"Why?" he gasped, horror ringing his eyes. "My library?" he almost whispered.

"Has been left untouched," she reassured him. "I only redecorated the livable parts of the house."

George sighed in relief. At least his citadel was preserved from this... this... whatever it was. "This is why you were so eager to get rid of me," he realized.

"Eager might be the wrong word, more like relieved."

"Why didn't you consult me on this?"

"You would have said no in no uncertain terms. So, I decided to act in your best interest, even if you don't like it."

Though not speechless, George didn't see any point in using words to describe how he felt. Instead, he wheeled his suitcase to his room (also reorganized) and fled into the library where he could be comforted by the familiar world he had built for himself. As tempting as it was to call his mother and demand to know whether she was an accomplice to this crime, he didn't, as he knew it be fruitless. Best case scenario, she'd laugh for about two minutes over the phone and, when she stopped, have nothing to offer but congratulations at having a home which didn't look as sterile as a spayed cat.

Opening his laptop, George accepted it was time to begin his book in earnest. The story wasn't quite there yet; he knew what he wanted to accomplish, but not quite how to do it. Much like breaking up his sister and Charles, he had the goal, but not the roadmap. With his morning pages, he sketched out a rough idea of character names he liked, the people and places, but he didn't know what the story would be. Like a pioneer or frontiersman, he would dare to seek out the unknown of the story from the wilderness of ideas.

Despite assuring Margaret he knew what he was doing, it only took three hours of staring at the screen and pacing around his desk to realize he had no clue what he was doing. A thought unaided by the phone call from his editor. Henry Newcastle had read the report generated by his announcement at the panel that week about the next book being a romance.

"George, don't take this the wrong way, but are you sure that's a project you should be trying?"

"Henry, would I try it if I couldn't succeed?"

A beat passed before the editor answered, "I've known you for a long time, George, and it's not your ability I doubt."

His cheeks flushed a touch. George was the author; he would choose what to write for his next book, not his publisher, and certainly not his editor. "Wait to pass judgement until you read the first draft," he insisted. "Then you can decide if it's worth more investment or not."

"When do you think you'll have the first draft?"

Eyes dancing between the two opposing bookcases on either side of him, George's mind flashed through his calendar, the target word count, and the boldness this project might necessitate. "I can have it finished for your birthday," he decided.

"By my birthday?"

"By your birthday, or soon after," George confirmed.

The phone call ended, and George was left to wonder if he hadn't just made a mistake.

"It's called research," George defended himself.

"It's called procrastination," Anthony corrected.

"When last I checked, I have freedom over my schedule. Why are *you* here in the middle of the day?" George asked sarcastically. "Could it be actual procrastination?"

"You're reading *Pride and Prejudice* in the coffee shop while the baristas fawn over you," Anthony observed. "When last I checked, you were supposed to be writing."

"It's called research," George argued again. "This is considered one of the best romance novels ever written, so I thought a refresher would be in order."

"It's called procrastination," Anthony repeated, sipping his latte.

"It's called a process," George maintained.

"I've got to get to work," Anthony announced. "I hope your 'process' gets you those pages you want finished."

They said their goodbyes and George was left again in the shop with thoughts of romance filling his mind. Compared to the way other people filled their minds with romance, he reasoned, his was a more productive state. His actually might lead to something marketable.

There was a trend of rewriting classics, giving them new titles and claiming the legacies of the original work, but that wasn't George's style. He preferred to tell a story cleverly enough no one would know what inspired it. It was why he enjoyed myths and legends; it was why today he was reading *Pride and Prejudice*. He rubbed his face. He just hadn't found a hook for this story yet. The characters didn't have any life yet breathed into them. Beyond the names in his pages, he couldn't see who they were or what drove them. He knew the overall theme would be the pursuit of love, but beyond that, it was still a mystery. The muse who had inspired the story was silent at the moment, waiting perhaps for him to stumble onto her next clue leading him down the path of the narrative.

George drank his caramel mocha and dwelt upon the mystery. There was no personal experience here to really draw upon; it was an area of life he had studiously avoided, the very reason so many had warned him away from the endeavor. Yet, romance couldn't be so hard to describe, could it? If he had the story, the driving element, he could bring it all together. The theme was there, and all he needed were the circuits to direct the power through.

These reveries were interrupted by a sight he had only ever seen in his nightmares: His mother had entered his coffee shop.

Mrs. Austen and Mrs. Stapleton breezed through the door and planted themselves at George's table. He chose to smile, despite it hurting, and greeted them warmly. "Why are you here?" he then added with a hint of desperation.

"You and Samantha come here often enough I thought I should drop in and take a look at the place. Agnes wasn't busy, and decided to join me in my conspiracies."

He gave Mrs. Stapleton a sympathetic look. "As long as your conspiracies don't involve me, I hope you two enjoy yourselves."

His mother laughed. "What an ego on this boy. Of course they involve you."

This did little to reassure George. He was beginning to feel trapped. Even if most of his home looked nothing like he left it, he could always run away to his library, where he'd be safe.

"Actually," Mrs. Stapleton said, "I was speaking to your mother and had an idea."

If every female figure in his life began to do this to him, he'd probably go mad. "That's kind," he said cautiously, "but—"

"You've got such a lovely voice, I was wondering why you haven't ever recorded the audiobook versions of your novels," she explained.

"A great idea," George admitted aloud. He set his coffee down beside him and steepled his fingers. As the relief at not being solicited to date a cousin's sister's niece flooded over him, he gave real weight to the question. Why hadn't he? His voice was a smooth baritone, easily one of the features which people complimented him on most frequently after meeting him in person. He had been told his voice had the everyman quality but was also resonant and active. It was a highlight to be able to give public readings of passages when on a book tour, so why hadn't he recorded the audiobooks? He needed to call his agent.

"Excuse me," he said to his mother and Mrs. Stapleton. Rising, he buttoned his sports coat, and exited. Completely immersed in his idea, he left behind not only a half-finished caramel mocha, but also the copy of *Pride and Prejudice* he had been reading.

"You've given him another distraction," Mrs. Austen chided her friend.

"He'll like it more than the one you would have suggested," Mrs. Stapleton defended herself.

"Maybe you're right," Mrs. Austen considered, taking her son's seat and picking the abandoned book. She flipped through the pages and saw the notes, the underlined passages, and a couple of the comments he made in the margins. "On the other hand, maybe you're wrong," she added hopefully.

It had been a few weeks since George had spoken to his agent. Frank Swashback was rarely consulted in regards to George's literary career; the bulk of his job was to manage the details George didn't want to. Show him which papers to sign and where. The announcement of the foray into the romance genre hadn't apparently worried the agent as much as the editor. Unless he just hadn't heard the news yet. George hoped the radio silence meant Frank simply trusted his instinct.

"Frank," George said to him now on the phone. "I have a question about audiobooks."

"George, good to hear from you. I've been meaning to talk about your next project."

So, Frank had heard the news.

"Before we get to that, I was wondering why I don't just read the audiobook for *Lord Wilmore*."

"You actually have perfect timing for this one. Normally we'd already have had it read and published along with the regular release of your book, but the guy we contracted got sent to rehab before the publisher could get it done. Now they're scrambling for someone to step in and get the job done."

"Sounds like the perfect opportunity for me to start," George noted.

"Just might be, but I'm not sure if they'll go for it."

"At least ask. If nothing else, they might be willing to have me narrate the next one."

"Right." Frank's voice became strained as he said, "Now, the next one. Let's talk about it."

"You've heard it's going to be a romance."

"Yes, but what's the plot?"

"It's a secret."

"I won't be able to get you an advance on this one," Frank warned.

"And I don't expect one. This is an opportunity to try something different."

"Different isn't always successful," Frank observed. "You can write a book that sells when you're alive, and you can write a book that sells when you're dead. I would rather you make the money while you are alive."

"Romance is a best-selling genre, and my *edition*"—George chuckled at his own pun—"to the genre will be a breath of fresh air when compared with the chemical manufactured rose scent the public is accustomed to."

Images of a dour, miserable, and overwhelmingly depressing commentary of romance sprang to Frank's mind. A tale of tragedy, not on par with *Romeo and Juliet*, but instead one that asked the reader to believe love is a polite fiction at the start, the middle, and end. He rubbed his temple in frustration. George could write well, but this...

"What's the plot?" Frank asked again. The silence he heard across the line wasn't encouraging. Half his job was to juggle the egos of the authors he worked with, but George usually wasn't a tough client.

Finally George admitted, "I don't know yet. I've got a half a notion, but not enough to make it worth explaining yet."

After an audible sigh, Frank said, "I can't tell you what to write or how to write it, but give me a manuscript and we'll find someone to publish it."

They exchanged farewells and hung up, leaving each stewing in their own relative dissonance from the conversation. What a difference, George noted, when you try to do something different from what you've always done. Everyone is comfortable with what you can do so long as you do the same thing again and again, but try something new and they sing a different tune.

It didn't take long to receive a call back from Frank. The publisher loved the idea of him recording the audiobook, but they were on a tight schedule, and needed him to drop everything and get to the recording studio they had booked for the next three days. "It's only a 225-page book," George said. "Why would it take three days?" After the first day, he was beginning to wonder if they shouldn't have actually booked it for four days more.

Dropping everything was easy enough; he hadn't been invested in the random scraps in his morning pages. Inspiration had yet to strike, and until it did, he considered this to be a productive way to occupy his attention. He was shocked at the striking difference between his voice at the start of the day and the version it mutated into by noon. The audio producer told him to take a break, and he would have them pick up again where he had begun to waver.

George could only nod in agreement. Here it was, definite proof against his family's claim he could talk endlessly. After a brief break he returned to the project again. The producer kept him on track and told him when he needed another rest. There were lines George would flub and need to re-record. Incredibly, he discovered definite sentences which appeared clever on the page, but were maddening to read aloud in anything resembling a commanding voice. Most of the characters didn't have any accents of note, but the ones who did, had accents he could manage. Thank you, BBC, he thought to himself.

George tried to read *Lord Wilmore* in the voice he had written it in, using the intonations which presented themselves as they populated onto the blank pages in front of him. Slowly, he began to wonder what voice would guide his as yet unwritten romance novel—but that brought him back to the project he was avoiding… er, researching.

"Remind me to thank Mrs. Stapleton for her suggestion, the place has never been so quiet," Samantha remarked, earning a glare from George.

His voice was weak from the three-day stretch to finish the recording. He was glad to be done with it. A great idea, though he had learned it required more preparation and recording time. Adding to his torment of the moment, he was "enjoying" dinner with his mother, Samantha, and Charles. It was his mother's idea, an opportunity for them to all get to know one another better. George had already made his judgement, and didn't see how more time spent with the man would be useful. Well, except as a way to learn how to get rid of him. As noble as his intentions were, it was hard to endure the man's voice, grating against his mind with every syllable.

"There's nothing more rewarding than seeing the smile on a child's face when you give them a bowl of rice," Charles related. "Everyone should go on a mission trip, it's an experience you never forget. The people, the place, the beaches there were amazing."

"I assume you've gotten involved in inner-city service projects then," George said hoarsely. Charles only gave him a blank stare, as if the very idea of helping people at home had never entered his mind. After all, how could he visit the beach by helping in Chicago?

The effort to speak was not worth it usually. Instead of commenting aloud, George had his commonplace book ready at hand to write down his replies. If he didn't, he was afraid the words would build in his head like steam until it burst. To allay any concern Charles wouldn't have someone readily able to support the conversation with, Mrs. Austen was promptly prepared to offer whatever thoughts or encouragements were needed to keep him talking.

"What an experience!" she remarked to Charles. "Those poor starving children, I can't imagine how we turn such a blind eye to them."

George noted in his book how people turn a blind eye to poverty not only in their own country, but even in their own state and county.

"I'd love to go on a mission trip," Samantha added wistfully.

George noted she complained when the hot water ran out. She wouldn't make it more than a day in a third-world country.

Blessedly, his cell phone began to ring. The number was unfamiliar. He recognized it was from Iowa, but it didn't matter. To get out of any further discussions, he would have answered if the caller ID read "telemarketer." Waving his ringing phone to excuse himself, George left the table and retreated to the library.

"Hello?" he rasped.

"Can I speak to George Austen?" a familiar female voice requested.

"Speaking," he replied with effort.

The voice laughed and said, "I'm not sure I'd call that speaking."

"Very funny, Margaret, how can I help you?"

"Very funny, George, that was my question. I hadn't heard from you about your book, so I asked Helen for your number to follow up."

George rubbed his forehead and wondered if he should change his number. "It's going fine."

"Is it?"

Dropping in his chair, George sighed.

"You sound like someone ran a cheese grater across your vocal cords," Margaret added.

"I recorded the audiobook for *Lord Wilmore*," he explained. "It was a little more effort than I anticipated."

Margaret giggled over the phone line. Resuming composure she asked, "How far are you with the new book?"

"It's still in development," he replied.

"It's still not started," she clarified.

"That's your interpretation of events."

"What's the sticking point here?"

"It's just a matter of waiting for the muse," George replied, shrugging.

"You're incapable of admitting you're struggling with anything, aren't you?"

"I was raised not to lie."

He could hear her eyes rolling through the phone.

"I don't know why you've got these hang-ups, but you shouldn't let them get in the way of telling a good story. Maybe all you need is a little experience in the topic. Instead of waiting to meet your muse, you should find her."

George greeted the idea with silence.

"That's the spirit!" Margaret said with a laugh.

George ventured a few polite questions about her life and her next project, and they talked long enough for Charles to poke his head inside the library to say goodbye. George gave him a polite wave and painted smile, then looked at the clock and said, "I've got to get going."

"You're welcome," she said with a laugh, and hung up.

George relaxed in his chair, secure knowing his home was once again free of pests and nuisances. Talking with Margaret wasn't the worst way to wait out the siege on his castle, but he did need to take steps to prevent it from ever being needed again.

Hanging up first was the right move. Margaret's mother had always recommended it as the best way to keep from looking like the idiot who's still talking. Tonight's conversation was good; it looked like everything was going to plan. The only part which had worried her was asking Helen for George's number. The fear she'd want to be involved in the strategy if she figured out Margaret's game. She didn't need Helen's help this time (except to get the number, of course). Whether it was because it served the plans she already had, or deciding it was the rational thing to do, Helen didn't ask any questions but gave the number up without comment. The reason didn't matter so much as the result. At least, that's what George probably would have said.

Rising from the couch on which she had been reclining, Margaret went to the washroom and started the bath. Bubble, bubble, toil and trouble, she thought as she chose which foaming bath soap to use that night. Yes, she was pleased with herself, and she had every right to be. In fact, she deserved a glass of wine tonight too. Maybe this was why Helen always looked so contented—to have a plan in motion and see it playing out precisely as intended. Margaret could play that game too, and she was quite sure she was going to win it. The enterprise had formed in her mind while they talked books over drinks. In an instant, she knew what to do and how to do it. Child's play, really.

The bubbles were a welcome reward, and the wine warmed the back of her throat as she meditated on the careful steps she had taken to get here. Admittedly, her plan wasn't complicated; but just as good books are simple, so are good plans. They don't ask the unreasonable and complex, they are straightforward in both substance and execution. George wouldn't know what hit him when the hammer fell. He would simply be crushed the same as anyone else. Clever words wouldn't free him, if he even thought to use them. Margaret sighed with satisfaction, listening to the small popping sound the bubbles made when she shifted, a chorus echoing her self-congratulations. One little doubt began to take root, however. She found herself unconsciously biting her lower lip as she considered it. Had she been too overt in her hint? She said to go out and find his muse—could it have been too direct a suggestion George should ask her out?

CHAPTER 7

I t was simple as adding words on a page. One letter at a time. George only needed to know what to say. The book, yet untitled, was still very much an idea, barely a single-cell organism. Margaret's interruption, while rescuing him from the torture of listening to Charles any longer, hadn't done much more than needle him about where he was in the process. Everyone thought he couldn't do it, and every time someone asked if he knew what he was doing, he said he did. Now, he was beginning to wonder if he really didn't.

One or two scenes he knew he wanted in the story had been scripted. He knew there would be an element of tragedy and heartache. It was the cost of love, after all, and should be an active threat to the story. He could see the protagonist left standing there like Bogart at the Paris train station in *Casablanca* waiting for a woman who would never arrive. His protagonist definitely needed to have a fedora too, a bit of texture to add old-school class and sophistication. Besides, fedoras looked cool.

After loafing for a day or two, drifting from the coffee shop to his library, and even walking, George didn't feel he was any closer to the plot of his story. To the hook which would draw him, and hopefully readers, to the narrative. He had reread romance novels of both the modern and ancient times, he analyzed the subject and medium, but it still eluded him.

"You've got to start writing," his mother announced, entering his library unbidden.

"Thank you, Mother," George replied sarcastically. "I was wondering how books were made, and you've just enlightened me."

"No need to be snippy." She sat down across from his desk. "You've decided to write a story you don't know how to tell, and I'm going to make a suggestion you won't want to hear."

"Fine. What?"

"Give it up and do something else."

"Not an option. I committed to this and I'll do it, and I'll do it to prove my point."

"So far, you're only proving why we thought it was a bad idea."

George's eyes narrowed at his mother, sharpening in intensity, but it wasn't a death glare, or even directed at her. He was thinking about the consequences, and his options. Something would break, he knew it.

"You should go on a date," his mother recommended. "It'll be just the thing to distract you, and who knows, maybe you'll even enjoy yourself."

There it was, the voice of the muse whispering in George's ear. Why hadn't he thought of it earlier? Here he was struggling to find the words to put on the page when the solution was nagging at him every time he turned around.

"You couldn't be more right," he said. "I'm assuming you have someone in mind?"

The lack of pushback surprised Mrs. Austen, but she wasn't about to look a gift horse in the mouth. Even if George recanted the decision later, she wasn't going to let him wiggle out of it.

"I do," she said. "Isabelle Johnson. She's the daughter of one of Mrs. Stapleton's friends. I'll arrange everything."

"Brilliant. Let me know when and it's a date," George said with a smile. Here it was, he thought. He could almost see the story getting its legs.

The following night, Mrs. Austen could barely contain herself. Rather than giving her son the chance to ignore her phone calls, she was waiting for him when he got home.

"Things went well?" she asked excitedly.

"Better than I hoped," George announced, striding to the study. "I couldn't have asked for more."

It was almost too much to hope for! George finally found someone who suited him, Mrs. Austen thought. Between Samantha and Charles and now George and Isabelle, she was beside herself with happiness.

"When are you seeing her again?" she prodded.

"No idea, don't know when we'd run into each other," George reasoned aloud, dropping into his chair behind the desk and writing in his commonplace book.

Confusion drifted across Mrs. Austen's face. "I thought you said you had a good time."

"I did. She gave me great ideas for the book."

As the pieces fell together, the illusion Mrs. Austen had created fell apart. Her son's interests hadn't changed a bit; he only found a new way of pursuing them.

"How..." she began, but left it alone. George was busy typing and probably wasn't going to say anything she wanted to hear. At least she still had Charles and Samantha to hope in.

As she was leaving George spoke up. "Mother, could you arrange another date for me with a new girl?"

Over the next month George went on two dates a week—dinner usually, sometimes lunch. Mrs. Austen kept alive an ember of hope he'd meet someone he liked through the process, but Samantha didn't believe it for a moment, and neither did George, if he gave any thought about it at all. The process had been better for research than George had expected. In fact, he was shocked to see how coherently the story was coming together. The plot was beginning to cement in his mind, the outline nearly complete. His method during a date refined over time; he would casually ask about past relationships and aspirations, and then prod the feelings of the moment and of course ask what they liked to read. Since they knew he was a writer, he would occasionally pass an idea he had for a story or scene past them. Playing out the bones of his narrative for their feedback. Not only did they find it flattering, but it provided him insight into how they responded to what he hoped to sell them later. After each date, he would review the notes he had made.

Date #1 Isabelle

Features: High cheekbones, sultry voice, rosy cheeks.

Personal weaknesses: Self-destructive, argumentative, a little vain.

Remark: Stabbed an ex-boyfriend in the leg with a fork when he broke up with her.

Conclusion: Messy in relationships, which are messy enough already.

Date #2 Daphne

Features: Blonde highlights (dyed), intelligent.

Personal weaknesses: Highly distractible, lacks self-awareness or anchor points.

Remark: Forgot what she ordered for dinner.

Conclusion: In a relationship needs to have her hand held the entire time to prevent from being run over by a bus.

Date #3 Megan

Features: Raven hair, porcelain complexion, witty.

Personal weaknesses: Has to one-up everything someone else says, a conversational narcissist.

Remark: Appeared distraught she could not one-up my trip to Paris where I met a descendent of Napoleon over dinner.

Conclusion: An overly competitive and self-absorbed nature which cannot abide anyone superior. Will find herself drawn to successful people, but frequently settle for less successful ones to make herself feel better until she can't stand them anymore.

Date #4 Victoria

Features: Sparkling conversation, fine features, piercing eyes.

Personal weaknesses: Incapable of silence, shares inane stories and talks about thoughts rather than actions.

Remark: Proves why authors are those who write, not those who just think.

Conclusion: Likely avoids risks for fear of failure; in a relationship would be reluctant to attempt anything which is not guaranteed.

Each date had a similar pattern of assessments. Occasionally, more details were added if George thought they might have a greater bearing on what he was looking for to write about.

After a dinner date, George was writing in the study. Tonight's date was talkative, and before any of the hastily made mental notes he had accumulated were lost, he wanted to get them recorded.

"Got a minute?" Samantha asked, entering the study.

George indicated the seat across from him, and she took it.

Looking at her brother, Samantha considered her words before she spoke. "You should have dinner with Chelsea," she decided.

"The same Chelsea who is Charles's sister?"

"Correct."

Weighing it a moment, he reasoned it wasn't a terrible idea. Not only did she like his writing, but it might give him an opportunity to learn more about how he could get rid of Charles. Though he hadn't forgotten his resolution to break up the couple, he had de-prioritized it in favor of the book. This might be a golden opportunity to further two plans in one evening.

"If you set it up," he said with a smile, "I'll be there with bells on."

"I was promised bells," Chelsea teased at dinner Saturday night.

"The expression has outlived the fashion." George laughed.

They were at the restaurant where they first met, when neither knew who the other person was at first sight. Chelsea was a classic girl next door, sweet as apple pie with a smile which lit up a room. Her features weren't what George would call classic, but fit her bubbly personality and lilting voice.

"I got an idea about what you were doing, and I want to help," she explained.

"Doing what?" he asked cautiously.

"Research, for your book," she replied matter of-factly. "You keep going on dates, looking for ideas for your book, and I want to help."

"Let's say you're right, why would I want your help?"

"Because eventually, you'll go out with a girl who likes you too much to let you go as easily as the others have. Then you've got a problem you don't want to deal with. If you just have dinner with me, you can get the same research without worrying about the risk of feelings becoming a problem."

"Your feelings won't become a problem?" he asked skeptically.

She laughed. "You are a charming man and I love your writing, but you are so not my type it's hilarious."

"I'll try not to take that personally," he said wryly.

"Don't, it's really not. I'm not a writer, but I think it would be fun to help you with this."

It was worth thinking about. After all, he had gone on dates with seven women so far, and it was enough to get the book started. If he tried this longer, the risk Chelsea suggested was a real possibility. Having the female perspective, beyond the two in his household and the teasing Margaret Clarke, would be useful.

"I'd even be willing to sign a non-disclosure agreement," she added with a smirk.

"Well, on those terms, I think we can come to an agreement," he decided, smiling.

The rest of their dinner went smoothly. He brought her up to speed on the essence of what he thought the story was at this time. How he had used the ideas from the dates he had already been on as compost to generate more ideas. "I'd like to make it like an ascension for the protagonist," he explained. "Each trial is like a Labor of Hercules. His ultimate winning of love must be born out of a struggle, but with the constant danger that very love places on him."

"What danger does love place him in?" Chelsea asked.

"All love is dangerous by nature. It gives an opportunity to be harmed when you could be safe, it's exposing the softest parts of who we are to someone else. Physical danger, no, but mental and emotional danger, yes."

"Don't take this wrong, but it makes sense you're single," she said sarcastically.

Since he didn't need to use every second of the evening to draw out ideas for his book, he turned the conversation to his second agenda.

"Charles and Samantha," he said, a prompt seeking a response.

"They make such a cute couple," Chelsea bubbled, causing George to realize she wouldn't be a willing accomplice in his endeavor. If she was going to be helpful, his attempts would have to be subtle.

"What was he like a child?" he asked. "I had a theory about how people who settle down together have similar childhoods, similar fears..."

"We were raised in classic suburbia, nothing too out of the ordinary. Charles was always talkative and bright. The only fear I really remember him having was... well, even now, he's afraid of guinea pigs."

"Really?" George replied with interest and amusement. It was a note worth saving for future reference.

"Really," she confirmed. "A student once brought their guinea pig into show and tell and it sent him running from the room screaming."

"It's hard when you're a kid."

"He was a teenager at the time." She laughed.

Yes, this was useful, and if he was being rational, Chelsea was good company. They had a pleasant rest of the evening, the conversation free flowing and the agenda falling by the wayside. He asked questions about what she wanted and how she felt, what books she had enjoyed reading and how they had inspired her. In sum, it was a charming evening.

Returning home, George took the notes he had made on paper, and the ones he had made in his mind, and found the basis of his female protagonist. She would be named Grace, with the same bubbly outlook as Chelsea and the same blonde curls and sparkling blue eyes. She could definitely be a threat to the heart of any man, and his protagonist, still a silhouette in his mind's eye, was nothing if not a man. The title itself materialized as he stared at his notes, a prompt edging from his memory of time long past. "But till all graces be in one woman, one woman shall not come in my grace," he said, quoting Shakespeare. In his notes, collected under the banner "untitled romance," he highlighted and replaced those words, typing "Until All Graces." Yes, the plot of his story had taken shape, and although he knew it would not be the same rivalry as Benedict and Beatrice, the attitude of the former must exist. It was one he could both sympathize with and relate to, and the best writing, he knew, came from a place of honesty on the page. Grace and the graces, being and virtues; he could see the interplay of the character and themes like wisps of fairy dust.

Smiling, George indulged in a moment of self-congratulations. In reflection, the arrangement with Chelsea would be profitable. She was playing the part of a muse well, and the inspiration was taking hold. George took a deep, self-satisfied breath and stretched in his desk chair. While not the most comfortable place to sit, it did its job and reminded him to not stay in it too long. A glance at the clock reminded him the day was well past done. Time to close up, let the ideas percolate overnight and return to them in the new dawn. He closed his laptop and was about to turn in when a soft knock came on the door. Samantha entered tentatively a moment after.

"Well?" she asked, an eyebrow raised.

"You knew what she was going to propose, didn't you?" George challenged, tapping his pen against the desk.

"Perhaps an inkling," Samantha admitted. "I knew what you were trying wasn't going to last very long, or very well. This is a better alternative."

"You were right," George agreed. "I think it's actually going to work out."

"Can't ask for more than that. I should be getting to bed, just wanted to see how my big brother's date went."

"Hold up." George stopped her. "How are things with you and Charles?"

Samantha thought about it a moment. "Good."

"You had to think," he observed.

"This feels real," she admitted. "I don't want to be overeager or under-serious about it."

He couldn't relate. It even irritated him a little she didn't see what a moron Charles was. How could she possibly want to keep him around? However, George knew that attitude wasn't going to win him any ground in this battle. Subtlety was needed where brute logic would not suffice.

"We should try to have dinner again," he offered, feeling the knife twist in his guts as he spoke.

"I'm sure he'd be up for it," Samantha said, beaming. "Charles says he thinks the world of you."

Of course he did. Now, George just needed to use it to his advantage. If the opportunity was there, why not put a little effort back into his agenda?

Just as he promised himself, George woke up early and, after a brief workout, put his focus on his now titled romance novel. For weeks it had felt like his creativity, energy, life force itself, was passively dripping away bit by bit. Now, there was direction. Now, there was a target to focus on. He did what writers do: write.

Over and over and over again, he set up tracks of sentences for his ideas to roll their way from start to the halting full stop a period made. It was exhilarating to be at it again. He made steady progress throughout the morning, barely noticing noon arrive and pass. The train of his words was only halted when he looked up from his pages to see Anthony Stapleton reclined in one of his study armchairs.

"Anthony, when did you arrive?" he asked with surprise.

"Oh, I haven't been here long," he reassured him. "I didn't see you at the coffee shop today, so I assumed you were holed up in here taking your coffee intravenously, maybe even writing."

"So you reasoned if I was productive, you should stop in and interrupt that productivity?" George summarized.

"As you're so fond of saying, that would be your interpretation of events."

"I had a breakthrough," George admitted. "My muse has spoken, and I know how the story looks."

"Does this muse have a name?" Anthony asked amusedly.

"Chelsea," George replied with mild reluctance.

"The same Chelsea who's Charles's sister?"

"The same."

George outlined to Anthony the agreement the two of them had arranged. He listened attentively, then gave him a schoolboy grin.

"I think it's the perfect opportunity for love to develop," he announced.

George blinked. "I think you missed the point."

"No, I understand it. I always thought you'd meet someone in your work. Granted, I thought it would be more the spinster librarian type, but Chelsea sounds far from that."

Before he could convey his disagreement, Mrs. Austen knocked on the study door and entered. "Samantha just told me how you're dating Chelsea now," she said, almost bursting with delight. "It's wonderful, simply wonderful. She's such a sweet girl, and you two make such a handsome couple."

Clenching his jaw, George counted to ten before speaking. "She's helping me with the book, nothing more."

"Whatever you say, dear," Mrs. Austen said, as if placating a small child. "Anthony, good to see you."

"You too, Mrs. Austen," Anthony replied, rising from his chair. "George, I'll leave you to your book and self-denial."

"You know me better than that. I never deny myself," George responded with a smirk.

Left alone with the beginning of his manuscript, he allowed a moment of doubt to settle. He asked himself if he wasn't flying too close to the sun with this arrangement. Juggling multiple women prevented feelings or attachment from forming, but could he maintain that disposition when it was the same woman? Yes, he decided. He was a rational person, and it that would keep him from forming any ill-conceived attachments.

As a child Margaret had started people watching whenever she was bored; as an adult it became a habit, and then a hobby. Writing required describing people, places, things, and ideas. Words were reflections of reality, and there was no better place for her to capture an image of reality than sitting on a bench in the Jordan Creek Mall and watch herds of people passing by.

It was surprisingly easy to deduce who was Iowan, born and bred. A similar German build was common, particularly in the rural elements. Easily contrasted with the more slight frames of the people who lived in the city. There was a slick blonde man walking past with an Express bag, probably containing the latest of hipster style with which to ironically dazzle his friends this weekend. A redneck with a thick neck passed her wearing jeans, boots, and Carhartt. Since he didn't have a shopping bag, she assumed he was headed to the sports store in the complex. She saw an older couple walking together in their golden years, white hair and thick glasses. Likely using the mall as an opportunity to stretch their legs until it warmed up a little more outdoors. It was actually kind of sweet in a way, but Margaret dearly hoped if she ever got married her golden years would never involve a shopping mall.

"I can't believe you wanted to meet up at the mall," Helen said, taking a seat next to Margaret. Her disapproval was evident, the disdain born not merely from an inherent snobbery, but the culture it typified.

"If you're going to people watch, you can't ask for a better screening," Margaret pointed out.

"I suppose it's why I will never be a writer."

"Among many more significant reasons, like writing," Margaret replied with a laugh.

"Brought something for you," the other said, dropping a newspaper on Margaret's lap.

"Really, an actual newspaper?" she asked, waving the paper.

"Just read it," Helen insisted. "Turn to the society pages."

Following her friend's suggestion, Margaret turned to the society page. It was a Chicago paper, and the headline was highlighted for her: "LOCAL AUTHOR IS A LOVE STORY?" The article described how George Austen, known as a secluded author (Margaret noted it sounded better than "antisocial"), had been seen on the dating circuit the last month with multiple different women. He didn't appear to have settled on anyone in particular, but sources close to him indicated this wouldn't be the situation for long.

The color rushed to Margaret's cheeks as she read. Apparently George had taken her hint, just not the way she had intended it.

"Thought you might find it interesting," Helen said. "It looks like George is warming up to people, and I have to say I'm shocked. This was unanticipated. Then again, I didn't think he'd ever write a romance novel either, so he's just been full of surprises lately."

Margaret didn't reply. She was too busy evaluating the possible moves on the board this news opened up. It didn't matter to her, Margaret told herself, it shouldn't matter to her at all.

CHAPTER 8

Spring

Finishing his word count for the morning, a self-imposed break was needed. George left his study and looked around the condo for Samantha, hoping to cajole her into joining him on a brief walk destined to end at the coffee shop. Yet, she was nowhere to be seen. He dropped her a text message asking where she was. A couple of minutes later, the reply arrived saying she was out with Charles. Another reason Charles needed to go, George reasoned.

Taking his walk alone ended up being useful, meditative even. He used the time to walk through the story he had so far, lining up mentally what happened next. It crossed his mind to tell Margaret Clarke he had come up with a title, but he decided against it. She could be impressed along with everyone else when it was completed and published. His attention needed to remain on the project at hand, the book which was not yet in being. It was his responsibility to breathe life into the story. His mother had always teased him that becoming an author was the only way he could exercise his God complex on the world, and he couldn't really disagree. It was his expression of deity, to create and write lives which appeared real. Of course, some might argue he couldn't give them souls, as

Margaret Clarke had at the writer's panel. What were her words? "Giving names to ideas." He chewed on the assessment as he walked. Alternating between defending himself and correcting the errors he was already making in the new book at the same time.

He concluded the walk by venturing into his home away from home, the coffee shop, where he was welcomed with the smiling faces of the baristas—and, of all people, Charles.

Samantha had said they were out together, yet there he sat, in *George's* coffee shop, at *George's* table, ordering from *George's* baristas.

"Charles," he said, painting a smile on his face, "what are you doing here?"

"Samantha said you like to hang out here, I had a few spare hours and figured, why not check it out," Charles explained, nudging out the seat across from him.

"Let me order and I'll join you," George almost choked saying.

"What can we get you today?" asked a more recent addition to the shop, Josiah. He was a young man with marginal ambitions, from what George could remember, but he made his mocha perfectly and only asked smart questions. He hoped the kid stayed on for a while.

"Josiah, I'll have the usual."

"Caramel mocha, hot, no whip," Josiah confirmed. "You've got it."

"Good man," George said, adding a couple of dollars to the tip jar. If there hadn't been a line behind him, he might have tried using a conversation with Josiah to delay joining Charles, but it couldn't be helped. Best case scenario, he could learn something to help him get rid of the man. He didn't want to consider the worst case.

"Is this what a writer's life looks like, coffee and free time?" Charles asked.

"Hardly," George corrected. "This is what you do while taking a break from writing, just like any other job." It was amazing how a question could be posed in such a way to get under his skin, intentionally or not. Others had asked similar questions that he usually didn't take as accusations.

"There's not a lot of free time for breaks in my job, always someone to help," Charles said, his voice convicted and strained. It was if the thought of people in pain wounded him physically.

"You're a chiropractor," George observed.

"Yes, and these hands, they heal people."

It was almost too much to bear.

"What first interested you in chiropractic?" George asked politely. He hoped Josiah could hurry with his coffee and he could escape while there was still a chance.

"It was when my mother hurt her back," Charles said piously. "That was when I knew it was my God-given role to heal the hurt others felt."

Where was Josiah with his coffee?

"Samantha is amazing," Charles added, suddenly changing the topic.

"I couldn't agree more," George replied.

"My relationship with her has been a highlight of my year."

It was in that statement George realized what he intensely disliked about Charles. He was possessive. Unconsciously or not, the man acted like he owned the world. It was proven in the way he treated both his own sister and George's. Charles acted like he was the biggest bull in the yard without reflecting on whether he actually was.

"My sister is exceptional," George said, leaving the words he wanted to say trapped between his teeth, then adding as an after-thought, "when she's not micromanaging."

"Micromanaging?" Charles asked, curious.

"You should see the way she plans something," George complained. "Everything has to be done her way and in her time. Surely she's done this with some of your dates?"

Sipping his coffee, Charles pondered the question. "She was very specific on where we've been meeting for dinner."

"That's also because she's a picky eater. Only eats a dozen different things. Mother and I were so grateful when she stopped eating chicken nuggets for every meal."

"That's actually a little sweet."

"At twenty it wasn't." George sighed. "Yes, she's exceptional, but not perfect by any stretch."

"Chelsea's been telling me some stories," Charles said uncomfortably, changing the subject. "Apparently the two of you have become an item recently?"

"She's helping me with my book," George explained, for what seemed to be the seventy-eighth time.

"Chelsea's not the kind of girl to fall head over heels right away, but give it time," Charles assured him condescendingly.

The world was not going to open up and swallow Charles, despite George's dearest hopes at that moment. Besides, risking any harm to his beloved coffee shop would make that choice regrettable. Maybe a convenient mugging gone wrong would be better...

"Here's your coffee. Caramel mocha, hot, no whip," Josiah announced, interrupting George's dark journey by delivering his order.

"Thank you, Josiah."

Puzzled, Charles said, "They didn't deliver my coffee."

A satisfied smile crossed George's face as he rose from his seat and said, "That's because they don't deliver coffee."

He left Charles in mild confusion. It was the least he could do to repay the man for leaving him in mild frustration.

Before getting back to the condo, George took a walk through the park. The weather was mild, reminding him spring was fresh as a newborn. Soon enough, he could spend an afternoon playing chess outdoors against anyone who was willing to take the risk. Although not a great metaphor for life, he enjoyed chess as an exercise of intellectual dominance. Very little hung onto luck or chance. Primarily, the game proved how quick you thought and how well you strategized (and studied). It was a discipline he had taught himself to get through a rough patch in the past, and he kept the habit going.

A few children played on the jungle gym while their parents watched their smartphones. Their squeals of excitement and delight added to the music of the day offered by the birds that were daring enough to be the first home. He took a seat on a park bench and removed his commonplace book from his jacket pocket. There, he noted a feeling which had passed through his heart, the emotion of a moment that he wanted to capture. It was the amusement of children being children in the outdoors, recalling to his mind those days he attempted to do the same as a child. Yet, he had always found it more fun to think about fun than to have fun. Vivid imagery conjured by his own imagination and the books he read supplied these moments, setting a stage for how he could occupy the real.

From his vantage point on the park bench, George could see a young couple walking together through the park. They were not arm in arm, but based on how closely they walked in step with one another, he assumed they were romantically inclined. If there was any doubt, it dissipated the moment he saw the woman smile. Her eyes were brilliant when they gazed at the man, dazzling in a way which left little question as to her feelings. The man was equally entranced, even almost tripping over a careless pinecone on the path. She helped him recover his footing before he could flatten, and the two laughed.

The pinecone was a good gag, George thought. He noted it in his commonplace book. From the time he had glanced down to write his note to when his eyes looked back up, the entire mood had changed. No longer were the two both smiling with face and eyes; now they were fiery. Anguish and frustration were read on their features, proving how easily passion can transform from one emotion to another.

The man began to walk away, shaking his head. The woman shouted after him, "No, you're not doing that, we're going to talk about it!"

Children and parents around the playground began to take notice of the argument.

"Not here," the man pleaded, trying to calm her down.

"Here and now!" she replied, her will ironclad.

"Fine!" the man shouted in return, any attempt to prevent a public scene over. "You want to talk about it, let's talk about it."

"I can't believe you said that," she hissed. "It was mean, it was wrong."

"You're taking this way more personally than you should."

"How else was I supposed to take it?"

"I don't know. You're getting bent out of shape over nothing."

"Don't even mention my shape!" she raged, his attempts at de-escalation completely missing.

"This is being blown out of proportion!" he insisted.

"You are a prick!" she yelled, and stormed away, leaving the man standing alone with a dozen small children, their parents, and George watching him.

Looking to heaven and letting out a deep breath, the man slowly walked toward where George was sitting and dropped on the bench next to him.

"I'm guessing you saw all that?" he asked.

"It was a little hard to ignore," George admitted. "But I noticed the two of you before things got hairy."

"Yeah, quite the change, huh?" the man said in wonder.

George was tempted to ask why and what happened—it was the interviewer in him—but instead he remained silent and watched the man. He noted the strain in the face, the confusion, the irritation underlying it all. Self-righteous in some way still, but edging towards repentance for what he didn't consider a sin.

"You want to know what happened?" he asked George.

"It's your business."

"It wasn't really anything."

"I'm sure it wasn't," George agreed, beginning to contemplate leaving and lunch.

"Just a misunderstanding," the man continued, "but she took it the wrong way."

"Clearly."

"You know what, it doesn't matter," the man decided, getting up. "We keep getting close to breaking up. Maybe this was just the straw which broke the camel's back." Nodding at George, the man left, leaving behind questions without answers and an anecdote for which George knew not the value.

It reminded him of how he had told Margaret the narratives of life aren't as clean or defined as the ones they wrote, how any attempt to put a story onto them tended to leave you with dangling elements you couldn't account for. On an impulse, he took his phone from his pocket and sent Margaret a text saying, "I've got a title."

Dropping the phone in his coat pocket, he rose from his seat and began the trek back home. By the time he had hung his coat in the closet, he received a message in reply.

"Are you going to keep me in suspense?" she asked.

"It's called *Until All Graces.*"

He didn't get a text back, and he shrugged. It didn't matter, shouldn't matter. It was time to get back to his plot, see if there was an opportunity to have his protagonist slip on a pinecone. Before he had a chance to take a seat at his desk, the phone rang with a now familiar Iowa number.

"That's quite a title," Margaret said without preamble.

"It's the one which suits the theme best."

"So does this mean you finally have a plot?"

"Wouldn't have a title if I didn't."

"Are you going to share with the rest of the class, or are you going to make me wait until I write a review?"

He could hear her smirk over the phone lines.

"I think you should wait in anticipation along with the rest of my adoring fans."

"What did Henry think, or are you waiting to tell him until tomorrow?"

"Tomorrow?" George asked, surprised. "What's happening tomorrow?"

"Helen said he was headed out to meet with you," Margaret said. "I assumed you knew."

George's jaw clenched. Normally, he didn't care; a surprise visit from Henry Newcastle would be welcome. However, he was suspicious about what prompted this visit.

"I didn't, but thanks for the heads-up, now I can make sure I have a bottle of his favorite red ready for dinner."

"Any luck on your auxiliary enterprise to break up your sister and her boyfriend?" Margaret teased.

"I may have laid some groundwork on that," George admitted, and told her about the horror of meeting Charles at his coffee shop, and some of the insinuations he made. "They were all true," he insisted. "I exaggerated a little, but not by much."

"Since you won't spill about your plot and haven't made any real progress on the plotting I know about, I'll leave you to it," she announced, hanging up before he had any chance to say goodbye. It was a pattern he was beginning to notice about her. She liked to end things on her terms instead of anyone else's, although maybe it was just her way of dealing with him. It didn't matter. What mattered was why Henry Newcastle was making a visit to see him unannounced.

CHAPTER 9

Margaret's prophecy came true the next day, with an early email from Henry Newcastle saying he was in town and wanted to see if they could meet for lunch. George wondered if he'd have felt different if he hadn't known in advance, what his reaction might have been if this email had met him as it was intended by the sender. The alternative reality didn't play out too far in his mind before he jotted out a quick reply saying it would be fine. They could meet at the coffee shop.

His editor was already comfortably reclined in an easy chair when George arrived, talking casually with Cassandra, one of his favorite baristas.

Behind the counter, Josiah was ready to take George's order. "We're going to change things today!" George declared.

"Shoot," Josiah replied, his expression as relaxed as ever. Occasionally George wondered if the boy was permanently stoned, but he never smelled like weed or seemed actually stoned. Just calm and relaxed, unflustered by anything.

"Let's have a straight black coffee," George decided.

"Dads everywhere are proud of you," Josiah quipped. "Have it right to you."

George took a seat across from Henry, crossed his legs, and smiled. "What a pleasant surprise! What brought you to town?"

"Actually, mostly to see you," Henry admitted.

"If this is a conversation you wanted to do in person instead of over the phone, it must be important," George reasoned cautiously. He briefly wondered what he would have noticed about Henry if he could read people like Margaret did. Would there have been any clues as to what brought this meeting, or would he only discover the man had an Egg McMuffin for breakfast?

"I have a proposal for you," Henry announced. "The publishing house is going to be publishing Senator G—'s biography and he needs a ghost writer. We couldn't think of anyone more capable to take that on than you."

Senator G— was among the few politicians George actually respected, and the rumor was he was preparing for a presidential campaign down the road. This book could be one of the building blocks to that end.

"Isn't that what speech writers are usually used for?"

"He asked us to pick the best, which is why we're asking you. Besides, he's a fan. Apparently *Lord Wilmore* was his favorite book from last year."

It wasn't an unappealing project. If anything, it presented an opportunity he didn't know the end of. As tempting as it might be to consider his next book before he finished this one, he didn't want to give himself any chance to call it quits before it was done. *Until All*

Graces wasn't likely to be a masterpiece or his magnum opus, but it was to date the most challenging thing he had attempted to write.

"I'd really like to wait to think about my next book until I finish this one," he decided.

Henry tightened his jaw and rubbed his neck. Finally, he said, "Actually, this would need to start now if you wanted it."

George narrowed his eyes. "And drop my current novel?" he asked suspiciously.

"Only postpone it," Henry insisted. "This isn't the kind of chance that comes up very often."

Leaning against the back of his chair, George steepled his fingers and weighed the matter. It could be a postponement, or simply a way of getting out of it all together. Why not? Didn't he hate romance novels? He had tried, and could say he had tried. Yet, he couldn't leave it there.

"It's a great opportunity," he finally said, "but I can't discard this book to work on the senator's. I appreciate the offer and the trust you have in me, but finishing my current novel has to be the priority."

Henry nodded his head, perhaps in resignation, perhaps in disappointment.

"George, I care for you like a son. So understand I want the best for you when I say take the offer."

"Henry, I can't. I have to finish my novel."

"Why? You've been hacking at it without progress. No one wants to read a romance written by a man, let alone one *you* write.

It's harsh, but it's the facts, George. You're clever with smart writing, but romance isn't a genre you should have dipped your toe in."

"Your confidence in me is overwhelming," George said sarcastically. "If I had known your naked thoughts were going to make an appearance I would have dressed more appropriately."

"You've used the phrase 'personal clutter' in the past. How should that fill me with any form of confidence you can write this and anyone will want to read it?" Henry argued.

"You are absolutely right, but I am a writer," George said, turning the phrase with the dexterity of a magician with a playing card. "My biases may come through in the book, I grant you, but more importantly my book will offer a perspective readers don't have on the shelves right now. Everyone writes about love and romance from the soppy viewpoint of a besotted melodrama. Mine will be one which prompts as much thought as feeling. More than empty calories, there will be some substance to my story. Besides, I finally have a title and plot."

"Fine. Let's hear them," Henry said exasperated, leaning back and drinking his coffee.

"*Until All Graces*," George announced proudly.

"And the plot is?" Henry prodded, less impressed than George wished.

"A playboy decides he won't marry anyone who does not possess all the graces, a challenge which he believes impossible until she walks into his life. Now, he has to win her heart, but she's unimpressed by his charm and charisma. He's forced to prove himself as more than a pretty smile."

"Not an original plot," Henry observed.

"No plots are original, everything is simply an iteration or alteration of a story people already know," George countered.

Even if Henry wasn't fully convinced, he appeared satisfied enough to let the matter drop. He changed the subject, asking after Anthony and Katherine Stapleton, Samantha and Mrs. Austen. It was polite chatter to avoid returning to the conflict.

"How's Helen?" George reciprocated.

"As chipper as always," Henry reported with a hint of sarcasm.

"What about Margaret Clarke?" George found himself venturing.

"Helen and she visit often, but I haven't heard much more than she's writing a short story for some anthology."

"She has the makings of an excellent author," George stated, drinking his coffee.

"Funny, I thought the two of you didn't get along very well," Henry observed idly.

"We made some form of peace after the writers' workshop we were both panelists for."

"Which reminds me, Helen was showing me some rather interesting rumors about you in the papers recently. Rather uncharacteristic of you."

"Only rumors," George asserted. "I was researching for the novel."

"Research?" Henry asked, eyebrow raised.

George recounted how a stroke of insight had given him the idea to use dates as fodder for his novel, kick-starting the writing process and getting him where he was today.

Henry nodded understandingly. "It's almost a relief to hear the world is still turning the way I expected it," he decided with a laugh.

"No worries on that score," George assured him. "To prevent any potential drama, a friend is 'dating' me while I work on the last few chapters."

Again, Henry looked puzzled, and George explained his arrangement with Chelsea.

"I don't know, sounds like you're actually dating someone, George."

"It's not like that," George insisted with a wave of his hand. "Purely a business arrangement."

"Do you still plan on finishing the book by my birthday?" Henry asked instead.

George smiled, the grin of the creative confident in his endeavor. "So far, it's a more than realistic projection. The book is forming better than I expected."

Henry's eyes narrowed on his protégé. "You seem to be looking at this as more than simply a lark?"

"It started that way," George admitted, "but it's becoming a story I'm really caring about."

"If you're turning down an opportunity to work with the senator, I sincerely hope you care about it," Henry scoffed with a shake of his head.

"We all take our risks," George agreed. "I'm taking mine. I hope you and the publishing house continue to take yours."

Grumbling, Henry nudged his nearly empty coffee cup back and forth on the table. "Is there anything I can do dissuade or distract you?"

"Not a thing."

"If that's the case," Henry announced, rising from his seat, "I will return to Des Moines. You've got a book to finish for me."

The two men shook hands and exchanged their farewells. George walked Henry to the door and returned to his seat, an idiotic grin on his face. His confidence was unchallenged and unquestionable. This book was happening, and it was all coming together. Through his efforts, an entire genre had the opportunity to become not only more interesting, but also more valuable. Yes, it might be the same basic story which had been told before, but he had no doubts he would tell it better than others had before. Insights people find valuable often come from seeing a similar problem in a different light, in a shift which causes them to examine their world again with a new perspective. George was ready to provide that perspective, whether the reader was ready for it or not.

CHAPTER 10

Summer

Months, weeks, days. Writing takes time. George could have broken the time farther down into the individual hours, minutes, and seconds, but he didn't see more value beyond remembering how many days it had taken. His word-to-day ratio had been good, putting him in a good place where he could spend an afternoon idly journaling in the coffee shop.

It was good to find some measure of success lately. His attempt to break up Samantha and Charles was less successful than he had hoped. Despite the lack of progress, he hadn't given up yet. Finally, he understood what his mother felt about his dating life. Briefly, he thought he had succeeded; Charles and Samantha had had a fight about her being controlling. The culmination of George's insinuation that she had the flaw of micromanaging—though Charles never mentioned his name. All it had taken was highlighting a habit, and Charles had begun to see it for himself, exaggerating it beyond the reality. Being so close to success, George had been disappointed to hear they resolved the matter. He should have known better than to think Charles was at heart a man who didn't want to be led by a woman.

There would be other chances, George hoped. For the moment, he was enjoying the satisfaction of another finished page and the anticipation of his caramel mocha. It was an anticipation which had lasted longer than expected.

Looking past his notebook and leaning to the side, he peered at the counter where the plebeians collected their coffee. No coffee was there. The day was quiet; only one other patron was in the shop, crouched on a stool in the corner wearing large headphones and huddled over his laptop screen like a gargoyle on a church's eave. No noticeable reasons not to have his coffee already. Rising, he crossed to the counter and looked for the delinquent barista.

"Josiah?" George enquired, rapping his knuckles on the wooden countertop.

Sitting on a stool, staring at his phone, Josiah didn't respond. Whatever he was looking at, he was all-consumed.

"Josiah?" George repeated, adding more weight to his voice.

This time, he caught the young barista's attention. His eyes rose from the screen and met George's in a melancholy gaze. "Sorry, I forgot your coffee, Mr. Austen," he apologized sheepishly.

Josiah sighed at the steamer as he made the mocha. It was a deep, wide sigh, which George assumed meant something profound and emotional he just couldn't care less about. Though he wanted to just walk away once his coffee was ready, he couldn't bring himself to do it. "Is everything alright?" he found himself asking.

"Well," Josiah began, hesitating. Apparently the weight of the problem lifted the reservations which held him back. "I need some romantic advice."

George raised an eyebrow. This may have been the first time someone asked such a thing of him. But why not? Josiah couldn't ask for someone more familiar with the topic than himself—wasn't his book coming along beautifully? "Join me at my table," George invited. "We'll talk about it."

Dropping the errant rag he had been wringing in his hands, Josiah followed George to his table and took the seat across from him. The two men looked at one another, the one confident in his ability to answer anything, the other filled with doubts. George chose to let Josiah start, to let him set the pace and ask the questions. He could clarify them and refine them into something more focused and useful. Heart questions appeared vague in the consciousness, as if in the process of feeling, the mind became incapable of isolating the material of the questions at play. It was the value of the second opinion, and the merit of asking someone who was bound to look at life rationally.

"There's a girl," Josiah finally started.

George nodded approvingly, waiting for more details.

"It's Cassandra," Josiah admitted reluctantly.

"Ah," George posited, "she's been working with you very much lately?"

"Much lately," Josiah repeated in a mumble. "She's so smart and clever, and hot, and I don't have a shot."

"Quite poetic," George reflected, ignoring the young man's woes to appreciate the sentence structure he had accidentally made.

"We've talked while we work. She's so... so..."

"Human, fallible, and just as prone to error as yourself," George supplied. "Don't make the mistake of setting Cassandra on a pedestal, it will elevate her beyond who she is and make it impossible for you to actually ask her out."

Josiah nodded wordlessly. George hoped the words were actually making a dent, but he wasn't going to take the risk they weren't.

"Take out your phone," he instructed Josiah. The young man obeyed and he added, "Create a note. I think you're not a pig I'm casting my pearls to, but given the emotions at play I want you to document in your notes app the advice I'm giving you. Otherwise it might not do you any good."

Josiah nodded, and began typing out the first instruction George had given.

Getting comfortable in his seat, George was prepared to lecture, to give Josiah the hard opinions and advice that no one else would offer. To tell him any romantic endeavor at his age was doomed for failure, how life was too short to waste it on people and relationships that had no chance of outlasting the warmth of his cup of coffee. But he found himself hesitating. A glance at Josiah's eager face, hopeful demeanor, and degree of desperation had him reevaluating. "Honest without being hurtful" popped into his mind. Damn, he needed to write that down to use in *Until All Graces*.

"Does Cassandra return your affection?" George asked, looking for a more detailed point to start with.

"Maybe?" Josiah replied unhelpfully. "We get along well, but she might just like me as a friend."

"Is only being her friend such a bad thing?" George asked. "Forget that, if she doesn't have a bias against you it's a good place to start. Virtually everyone you meet is looking to be swept off their feet, they just don't know who the one who's going to do it is. They want love and romance in their lives, and they want to be surprised by it, even if they claim differently. I caution you to manage your expectations. The odds are always against you, but that's the value of trying something different. You win, you win. You fail, you tried."

Josiah nodded, so George thought he was on a roll and kept going.

"Before the feelings get worse, because they most definitely will, just ask her out to anything but coffee, and use those words. Given your context, she's used to coffee and will appreciate the novelty of something different. Get it done. Get it done sooner rather than later, and don't be a bloody creep about it."

"Don't be a bloody creep about it," Josiah repeated, typing the directions onto his phone.

"Tearing the Band-Aid soonest is best," George reiterated. "The longer it draws out, the worse it will make you. If she says no now, it will hurt far less than when... *if* she says no later."

Josiah's head bowed in frustration. "This isn't what I expected," he sighed in exasperation.

"It never is," George agreed, banished memories brushing against his mind. Gritting his teeth, he pushed them back. He was the rare event, the person who chose to change the rules before they could change on him. He'd never let himself be where Josiah found himself today, not again.

"You'll be tempted to tell yourself a story, don't. Let the story tell itself," George cautioned in a hard voice.

Josiah nodded in what George hoped was understanding. If nothing else, maybe next time Josiah would deliver George his coffee without needing to be reminded. The bell at the door rang, and a new customer entered, forcing the barista back behind the counter after thanking George for the advice.

"Tremendous timing," Chelsea said, taking Josiah's vacated seat. "What was that all about?" She had just entered the shop following the door-ringing customer, and delicately took her place across from George, right on schedule to review his current notes for the polishing work on the manuscript.

"Nothing much, just making sure I keep getting my coffee," he replied, indicating his beverage.

"Any chance you'd be willing to do that for me?" she asked sweetly.

Nodding, George rose and ordered Chelsea's coffee. In the duration of their acquaintance he had learned her order: an iced caramel latte. The first time she had asked for it he had balked; iced coffee always rubbed him the wrong way. But, Chelsea's opinions had been helpful, and as she was spending evenings she might have been looking for an actual partner acting as his for the sake of his book, swallowing his pride to order her an iced coffee was the smallest kindness he could perform.

"Your girlfriend hasn't been in here very often," Josiah observed.

"Chelsea's not my girlfriend," George assured him.

Josiah only nodded and made the iced coffee. The question had come up more than once at this counter, prompting George to wonder if the baristas were confused or he was. He knew which he thought.

Settling in across from Chelsea, he passed her the coffee. She had been admiring his journal, a leather-bound book with crisp acid-free pages and a bookmark. "Any chance I'm noted somewhere in there?" she asked teasingly.

"Maybe once or twice," he admitted, "but I'm happy to announce our little project has drawn to a close. The first draft is nearly finished and I don't see why we need to keep going out now. Thank you, your ideas and company have been very valuable for the book."

"Am I going to get a shout-out in it?"

"In the acknowledgements," he assured her. "You've been a big help. In fact, I'd like to invite you to come to Henry Newcastle's birthday party in Lake Geneva."

"Really?"

"Why not? Samantha is inviting Charles, and I'm going to enjoy having a brief break from the book."

"You don't seem like a person who vacations," she observed. "Besides, won't it be intruding to have a stranger there for his birthday?"

"I'll be putting some finishing touches to the first draft," he admitted, then added, "Henry's birthday parties are legendary. Over three hundred guests at his lake home—an estate, really. It's an event. You won't be the only stranger there."

Tilting her head, Chelsea gave it more consideration than George thought was required, but ended up nodding. "It'll be fun," she decided with her usual bubbly enthusiasm. George hoped she was right.

CHAPTER 11

George had heard Lake Geneva referred to as "the Hamptons of the Midwest," and by Midwestern standards, he couldn't disagree. Lake Geneva was the ideal destination in Wisconsin for enjoying a warm summer day, particularly if you knew someone who was letting you use their lake home. He didn't want to think how much the taxes on a place like this cost the Newcastle family, but it was an expense Henry was happy to maintain even only to use it a couple of times a year. Apparently it was a useful enough investment to park family money for them. George wasn't about to complain; he had a set of keys to use it whenever he wanted.

Unlocking the door, George dropped his keys in the shallow glass fishbowl next to the door. It was an ugly green. He had debated dropping it in the garbage can or hurling it into the lake the first time he saw it. Now, he viewed it like an outspoken mole on a friend's face. You just got used to it.

Not long after he arrived, George heard the sound of car doors opening and closing. Looking around at the empty living room, he enjoyed a final moment of solitude. He would survive the upcoming week around family and friends—and Charles—but he promised himself a week of isolation in the future. The party was enough to make up for the minor inconveniences. It was hard enough to get away with driving up to Wisconsin alone. His mother had been appalled he didn't at least take Chelsea with him, to which George replied with the now tired refrain, "She's not my girlfriend."

No matter how often he repeated the phrase, it still didn't seem to sink in. At best Chelsea was a friend. A friend who had just arrived.

"Great place!" she bubbled, looking around at the grand old home.

"You'll have a chance to compliment the owners when they get here," George replied. "Do you need help with your bags?"

"I've got them, but I think your mom wants help with groceries," she said. "Which room did you take?"

"The first-floor rooms are numbered, the second-floor are alphabetical with numbers, and the third-floor are the suites, which are named after authors. I'm in Room 3A."

"He hasn't named a room after you yet?" Chelsea joked.

"I offered."

Leaving Chelsea to wander the halls, George dutifully carried the groceries for his mother from the car to the kitchen. He noted with some irritation Charles didn't seem the least interested in volunteering to help, but he wasn't about to ask him to. Carrying all the bags himself was preferable to listening to Charles.

Once everything that had been outside made it inside, George decided to settle on the porch. Closing his eyes, he took a deep breath of the lake air. It didn't matter the distinct aroma was caused by seaweed and dead fish, it was still relaxing. For the moment, he wasn't thinking about his book, his plots, or how he was going to tackle the next hill. Right now, he was enjoying the warmth of the sunshine on his face and the lake smell. All was right.

"You should wear sunscreen if you're going to tan out here," Charles said, shattering the serenity.

Opening his eyes, George saw Charles take the seat across from him. Dressed in khaki shorts, a sporty polo, and sunglasses, Charles looked ready for a day by the lake. His face also looked about three degrees lighter in complexion from the layers of sunscreen he had added to it. With peace no longer an option, George debated taking up war, but was interrupted by Chelsea appearing through the sliding door.

"That's a great bikini," Samantha remarked, popping out from behind her in a simple one-piece.

"Thanks!" Chelsea said, tossing her head a degree. "What do you think of it, George?"

While it wasn't the skimpiest bikini George had ever seen, it did flatter Chelsea's figure in all the right ways for optimum attraction. Rationally speaking, of course. "It's very becoming," George decided, and began to wonder if he shouldn't get his own swimsuit. After all, a tactical retreat might be the best move at the moment.

Swimsuited up, with a Sea Island cotton shirt, George ventured again outdoors to the patio. Happily he observed Charles had relocated to the yard, where he was helping Chelsea and Samantha set up croquet. The little white tunnels were sprouting like mushrooms in the grass.

"You should play with them," his mother proposed, joining him on the patio.

"You said the same thing when I was ten, and like I said then, I prefer to read," he replied, waving a paperback book he had been trying to find a few moments alone with.

Mrs. Austen rolled her eyes. "If you're at the lake, you should enjoy yourself."

"And I am," he insisted, again waving the book. "Last time I was here I was writing, I was alone and enjoying the quiet and solitude. Now, here again with all of you..."

"You're enjoying the company," Mrs. Austen finished for him.

"Something like that." He sighed.

Mrs. Austen released a deep breath, sat down on one of the chairs, and gave her son an affectionate smile. "You could do worse than Chelsea," she said.

"Let's not have this discussion." George said flatly, opening his book.

"I think you're going to need to have it at some point," Mrs. Austen observed. "The girl said she wasn't going to get emotionally invested in you, but are you sure? You did invite her here, after all. Maybe you're the one developing a little emotional attachment?" she pondered hopefully.

Shutting the book, George rubbed his temples. This wasn't a conversation he wanted to have. To make matters worse, he should have expected it. What was he to tell her? How could he explain the simple fact he didn't care about Chelsea in that way? All feelings are dangerous, but the dreaded L-O-V-E kind are the worst.

"Don't waste time here arguing with me," his mother advised. "Just think about it instead of pushing it away immediately."

"Mother—" he began.

"Don't try smooth talking, you need to be honest with that girl or honest with yourself."

"I haven't led her on," George insisted.

"I'm more worried about you leading yourself on," Mrs. Austen cautioned. "You don't need to discuss this with me, just think about it."

George growled in response. This wasn't what he had planned on doing with his vacation. Leave it to his mother to find a way to make playing croquet seem like a good idea.

The game was pleasant enough—pleasant until Charles became as insufferable as a rock in George's shoe.

"You'd be a great croquet player if you would work on your ankle mobility more," Charles advised him unnecessarily.

George grit his teeth, tempted to say it was unwise to criticize a man who was holding a mallet within swinging distance of you, but he restrained himself. Instead of hitting Charles, he struck his red ball perfectly through the hoop, finding its stop nestled against the pole.

Despite his comments, Charles wasn't a much better croquet player. He always managed to strike with the edge of the mallet, and that worked only about 20 percent of the time in his favor. Whenever he missed the mark, Samantha would say something encouraging and George would think of something snarky. Chelsea was the most invested in the game, which may have had something to do with the fact she was winning. George suspected that's why she was ignoring her brother's comments. Chelsea's competitive spirit was in full tilt, and she was determined to give no quarter.

Looking wistfully at the boathouse, Samantha asked, "Can we go out in the boat?"

The Newcastles had the powerboat and piers added and removed by a local marina every year, and as far as George knew, it was ready to go for the summer. "Sure," he decided, "I'll get the keys."

"I'll pilot," Charles volunteered. "I had to drive a couple of these up- and downriver when I was working on a project to bring fresh water to children in Nigeria."

Lake Geneva was the second deepest lake in the state of Wisconsin. For a brief moment, George fantasized about chaining Charles to the bottom of it.

They spent twenty minutes touring around the lake, enjoying the sunshine, even pausing to swim. Samantha, Chelsea and Charles all dove into the water. George elected to remain in the boat with his book. Wearing a pair of sunglasses to cut the sunny glare from the white pages, he quietly enjoyed the perfect way to read on a summer's day. The sound of water splashed next to him, along with a wet plop that he ignored, keeping his eyes glued to the page. "Aren't you going to swim?" Chelsea asked.

"I'm enjoying my book," George replied. "I can swim later."

"You could also read later," she pointed out.

He shrugged and returned to the book.

Chelsea settled comfortably into a seat. "What are you reading, anyway?"

"It's called *Tales through Time,* a short story collection. A couple of them are really good. Each author writes a particular story for a different generation, giving the reader a perspective of several lives over the last two hundred years."

"Did you write any of them?" she enquired. By now she had decided to start sunbathing and was applying sunscreen to her lithe figure.

"No, I didn't have anything to do with the project, although it's a fun idea."

"Which generation would you have wanted to write about?"

George thought a moment, running the archetypes through his head and finally deciding, "Someone who lived in the Jazz Age into the Depression. But I'm guessing that was the one most of the authors would have wanted to write about."

"I think the Gilded Age would have been interesting," Chelsea remarked. "A time America forgot."

It was a keen insight. Bubbly and affable—and attractive—as Chelsea was, people could easily ignore her mind if they didn't take a few moments to talk to her seriously. It was one of the reasons she had been so helpful on his novel. Their conversations hadn't been labored like he anticipated, but easy and free. Free in a way he was coming to appreciate. There was no expectation or motive; at least, there never had been. Unexpectedly, he found himself watching as she applied the sunscreen. Catching himself, he cleared his throat and announced, "I'm going back to my book now."

After Samantha and Charles had enough swimming, and Chelsea had enjoyed enough of George's silent reading, the company returned to the Newcastle home. Trolling slowly back to the dock, Chelsea began teasing George again for spending more time engrossed in his book than in talking to any of them.

"I don't know how you read in the boat," she said, exasperated.

"George could read in the middle of a hurricane," Samantha interjected with a roll of her eyes.

"It's the perfect way to relax," George insisted.

Sitting next to George, Chelsea gave Samantha a mischievous glance and, with surprising speed, snatched the book out from his hands. She then waved it in the air like a taunting child.

"Surely we're more mature than this," George said, extending his hand for the book to be returned. Instead, Chelsea kept it out of arm's length.

George reached further, and his balance was off just enough, Chelsea saw her opening. With a quick push, George was out of the boat and in the lake.

"Oops," she said with a smirk and a wicked wink.

Bobbing up, George rubbed the water from his eyes. "Not funny."

"You might as well swim back to shore, we're so close," Samantha suggested, even as Chelsea extended an arm to help him back into the boat. Descending into adolescence himself, George used the chance to pull Chelsea into the water with him. She let out an excited squeal as she dropped, leaving Samantha and Charles laughing in the boat.

Not one to let a competitive moment pass, Chelsea shouted, "Beat to you to the shore!" and began swimming.

George followed, determined to make a point. She yelped as he caught up, scooped her up in his arms, and carried her onshore. "I think I won," she insisted with a laugh. Gently setting her down on the beachfront, George said nothing. He stared at the woman standing in front of them. She had brown doe eyes and auburn hair.

"I think it's a draw," Margaret Clarke decided.

CHAPTER 12

I t was precisely the time away Margaret had been looking for, the break she needed, and maybe even the chance she had been waiting for. The invitation from the Newcastles had been unexpected, and she had never been to Lake Geneva before. The opportunity to attend Henry's birthday party would be amazing. She was quickly packed and ready. When she heard George Austen was going to be there, she made sure to pack a few dresses she might not have otherwise, along with what she thought was a fetching swimsuit. Could George's attention be caught with the right clothes, or lack thereof? Possibly, for all the bluster he poured out, he was still just a man.

Yes, a man indeed. Standing there on the beach with a blonde in a bikini whom he had just carried out of the lake. Margaret had walked there to enjoy the view—a plan which had immediately soured.

"Chelsea Parker, Margaret Clarke," George introduced the two.

Margaret tried not to wince at being placed second in that order. "Pride got no one anywhere," she repeated in her mind.

"I didn't know you were coming out here." George said, shaking her hand, and giving what Margaret hoped was a smile.

"It was a last-minute invitation." Turning to Chelsea, she added, "It's a pleasure to meet you."

"You also," Chelsea said in a voice which reminded Margaret of soap bubbles. "I'm going to get a towel." And she walked up the yard.

Now here the three of them were, sitting on the patio. George and Chelsea on the love seat, Margaret on the opposing chair. It seemed to Margaret the other two were sitting rather close to each other, Chelsea seemingly at ease being half naked with less than a half inch of distance between herself and George.

"Chelsea, tell me about yourself?" Margaret asked politely.

"I'm an undergraduate at Lake Forest University," Chelsea explained. "I'm getting my degree in sociology."

"Margaret's also a student of people's behavior," George added. "A gift she's applied to adding more good books to our shelves."

"How did the two of you meet?" Margaret asked, partly out of curiosity, partly out of frustration.

"She's my sister," Charles said, joining the conversation uninvited and sitting in the chair next to Margaret. "You might say I fixed the two of them together."

It took only a moment for Margaret to realize this was the man George had decided needed to be disposed of. The brother who had offered up his sister at dinner. Had George taken him up on the offer?

As if to answer the confusion which must have passed over Margaret's face, George explained, "Chelsea's been helping me with research for my upcoming book."

"Research... right," Margaret thought.

"Hello everyone," Helen Newcastle announced, making her entrance onto the patio as if it were a Parisian salon. She had on a white sleeveless dress, sunglasses over her coal-colored eyes, and a smart white hat on her dark hair. Gracefully she seated herself on the ample space unused on the loveseat and introduced herself to the newcomers.

"Chelsea, aren't you charming?" she said with a smile resembling a shark examining prey. Margaret watched George's reaction. There was little question in Margaret's mind Chelsea was being sized up as a chew toy unless George made a move to stop it. If he did, that would tell her a lot about where the two were in relation to one another.

"Charles, Helen has been debating taking a mission trip to Africa for ages. Would you mind telling her what she can expect?" George asked.

With this license in hand, Charles excitedly began to relate more details about the beaches and sightseeing one could enjoy than the children one could help, starving or otherwise. Margaret could see the genius of the question. It instantly redirected Helen's attention from the sister to the brother, a man who was sufficiently boorish. There was little doubt Helen would find a way to make George pay for wasting any moments of her life listening to him. How was Margaret supposed to interpret that move?

"Well, my little people-reader, what do you think of the newcomers?" Helen asked Margaret. The two girls had retreated to Helen's room as she was unpacking her suitcase and Margaret had taken to pacing back and forth in front of the bed as Helen calmly removed items from the luggage.

"Chelsea is a bimbo," Margaret decided. "She has a food allergy but isn't attentive enough about what she eats to be aware of it, her exercise routine needs to be changed, and she's really too comfortable wearing too little. She's used to having what she wants and gets away with it because of her looks. Anytime she's posed with a challenge she finds someone else to do the work for her. She expects to be placed on a pedestal."

"All that from her bikini?" Helen asked. "Impressive, but maybe stretching it."

"Her bikini could have stretched more," Margaret muttered.

"Why do you care? The brother's the bore."

Helen watched her friend a moment. She didn't possess Margaret's capacity to read people, but she had a clever mind. All it took was the right seed, and the growth was instantaneous. "You like George," she realized, smirking with surprise. "Why didn't I figure it out sooner?"

Margaret didn't have to say anything to confirm the theory, but she managed, "It was one thing when the reports said he was dating a bunch of girls. Now if it's only this one, it's a lot harder."

Helen stopped unpacking and sat down on the bed to give Margaret her complete attention. Things were serious now. "Why didn't you tell me?"

Margaret kept pacing and replied, "With the history the two of you have? It didn't seem like a good idea."

The illusion adults were better at managing their feelings than teenagers was just that, an illusion. As much as Margaret wanted desperately not to sound like a teenager embroiled in high school drama, that's precisely where she felt she was at.

"You could have told me," Helen insisted. "I could have helped."

"Really? Like you helped at his dinner party when you used me to swipe at him?" Margaret lashed.

Helen shrugged. "I know George better than you. I might have been able to give you some advice."

"Like how it's a flawed strategy and I would be better off being interested in someone else?"

"Possibly," Helen said, musing. In retrospect, she was surprised it didn't click sooner. Given her knowledge of Margaret, it made sense she'd find George Austen attractive. Beyond simply seeing people for who they were when she "read" them, Margaret had a capacity for seeing who they could become. For whatever reason, she saw something in George that prompted her interest and attention. "How could I help?" Helen asked, pondering the question in her mind even as she spoke.

Spent by the pacing, Margaret collapsed onto the bed next to Helen and sighed. "I'd rather you didn't. It's a schoolgirl crush, nothing more. He's got Chelsea, and there's no reason I should try to interfere with that."

Helen couldn't help but laugh. "You think he and Chelsea are an item?" She nearly snorted.

"Of course they are. Look at the two of them together."

"My dear friend, you may be apt at reading people, but I know George. He's not interested in her. She probably has some fascination with him, but he doesn't have romance on the mind at all when she's around," Helen said authoritatively.

"He's comfortable with her," Margaret challenged.

"Which you can just as easily say about yourself."

Margaret thought a moment, biting her lower lip. She was searching for how to phrase this question without sounding pathetic, but finally gave up, asking, "Do you think he likes me?"

"You already said you don't want my help, so I think you need to find the answer on your own," Helen decided. Rising, she returned to unpacking her clothes, the amusement of the situation still dancing in her head. If George knew, it would be enough to make his head explode.

After dinner, Charles, Chelsea, and George were playing croquet with Henry Newcastle and Mrs. Austen. The sun had only started descend, giving a beautiful view from the patio where Samantha, Helen, and Margaret stood talking. Mrs. Austen stepped outside and joined the girls. "I've been coming to Lake Geneva since I was a little girl," she said wistfully. "Years of wonderful vacations have been spent here."

"I'll bet you've got some great stories from over the years," Margaret observed.

"Oh, too many," Mrs. Austen replied with a laugh. "My favorite is from just a couple years ago though. George and Cynthia had—"

"Mother!" Samantha interrupted, quickly looking to see George wasn't nearby. "He'll hear you," she whispered.

"It's been four years, I'm sure…" Mrs. Austen began.

"I'm sure Margaret doesn't need to hear about ancient history." Samantha interrupted again, "As a matter of fact, we'd love to hear about what you've written recently," she said. The abruptness of the change of topic surprised Margaret, but she went along with it. As Margaret was about to answer, George discarded his mallet and joined them, Chelsea following after him like a puppy. They sat down opposite her near Samantha.

"I'm still working on the outline of my next novel," Margaret explained, "but I did write a short story published in an anthology."

"What was it called?" Samantha asked.

"*Tales through Time*. I wrote about a generation of Jazzy reprobates who learn their lessons in the Great Depression."

"That's the book you were reading yesterday on the boat!" Chelsea said, pointing at George. "What a coincidence."

George seemingly ignored the comment, focusing his attention on the drink in front of him. Margaret thought she could detect the hint of a blush edging his cheeks. What a coincidence indeed.

CHAPTER 13

I t wasn't a coincidence George was reading the anthology Margaret
had contributed a short story to, but there wasn't a chance under
sun, moon, or stars he would admit it. He noticed Margaret's glance
his way, which he chose to ignore. Worse, he could see curiosity light
up Helen's dark eyes. But that was a matter of little consequence,
and as such merited no comment on his part. How to change the
topic passed rapidly through his mind, but it was an unnecessary
worry. Everyone's attention was drawn to someone joining them on
the patio.

"George Austen!" the newcomer exclaimed.

For the love of all that was holy, George couldn't imagine why
Paulo was there.

Paulo Castillo, professor at the University of Iowa and author
of a yet unpublished masterpiece, was standing on the patio in front
of George.

"I appreciated the invitation," Paulo said, seating himself far
closer to Margaret than George expected. "I brought with me some
fine wine to enjoy during the vacation," he added happily.

For a brief moment George pondered if Paulo had assumed the only way to survive his company for an extended period of time was to have an elevated blood alcohol level, or if it was just an attempt at a pleasant gesture.

By this point, Chelsea was leaning against George, but thankfully she was dry enough he wasn't bothered by it. She glanced up at him with an expression which begged to ask, "Who's this bozo?" Well, maybe "bozo" was his addition to the translation.

Samantha politely welcomed Paulo, which the professor took as license to tell everyone how his book was coming along.

"I'm at the point where the hero is about to pass from the extraordinary world back to his homeland, but he hesitates, because he knows there is more to do," Paulo began, and then proceeded to relate how he pained and agonized over how long the hero would remain in tribulation before he attained the prize he sought. He compared the plot to the Labors of Hercules, the Trojan War, and the biblical Exodus from Egypt all at the same time. "It is epic in every way," Paulo repeated three times over the span of his monologue.

Glancing at Helen, George saw her eyes widen—with shock or astonishment, he couldn't tell. Turning his attention to his drink, he determined there wasn't enough whiskey left in the glass to listen to any more of this. Paulo's hot air had even melted the ice.

"I'm going to get a drink," he announced, rising.

"I'll join you," Chelsea said, hopping up behind him. "I'll grab a sweater too, it's getting chilly." George had been a little surprised she had lasted this long in just her bikini, but it wasn't his place to comment.

"Who's that?" Chelsea asked once they were in the kitchen, out of earshot.

"The beginning of alcoholism," George said, pouring two fingers of single-malt whiskey into the rocks glass. He gave her a summary of his experiences with Paulo at the panel and how he and Margaret had joined him for drinks at a local piano bar afterwards.

"Why is he here now?" she asked, confused.

"I have the same question," he said, leaning against the counter sipping his whiskey.

"He and Margaret seem close, maybe they're dating or something," she suggested with a shrug.

The whiskey nearly came back up. George didn't know which idea would appall him more: them dating, or *something*.

"How long have you known Margaret?" Chelsea asked, leaning against the counter with him.

"A little longer than I've known you. It was partly due to her I started writing *Until All Graces*."

"How so?"

"A review she wrote. It challenged me to write the feelings of people, not just the ideas. More specifically, romance. A topic which she knows I avoid both professionally and personally."

"I don't know," Chelsea said after a moment's thought. "We've been going out for a while for 'research,' and I think you've been pretty romantic."

"That's kind of you to say," George replied, holding the glass to his temple. For a brief moment, he thought he heard an alarm in the back of his head, but he ignored it. Faintly it sputtered, and he just took another sip of his whiskey. Nothing more than the strain of having Paulo and Charles in the same zip code at the same time, he decided.

"Let's get back out there," he said.

"Sure you don't want to just head to bed? You look beat," Chelsea observed.

George clenched his jaw. Maybe it was the writer in him, the part which wanted to see how events played out. He couldn't leave before the show was over. More to the point, he didn't want to go to bed wondering what was going to happen next. FOMO, or fear of missing out, was what some people called it. He didn't think such labels could apply to a rational person, because those fears were born of irrational outlooks. He was different, he was rational; he just wanted to know what happened next.

Before Chelsea and George could leave the kitchen, Helen entered. Direct as ever, she said nothing to either of them as she reached for a glass and began to fill it with a dark red wine.

"I'll catch up with you in a minute," George assured Chelsea.

Nodding, Chelsea scampered away without a comment.

"She's cute," Helen observed, turning to face George with an amused smile.

"We aren't having that conversation," George replied, giving her a look which meant every word. "Instead, I want to know why Paulo is here."

"You're asking the wrong person." She took the first sip of her wine. "But," she added, "he was just telling us how he was delighted to receive an invitation to the party. Apparently he heard family and friends were arriving early and assumed he was counted among them."

"Of course he did," George sighed, taking another drink of his whiskey.

A mischievous expression played on Helen's face. "If I'm reading the situation correctly, Paulo had invited Margaret to carpool to the party this weekend, and she let the cat out of the bag." She mused with pursed lips.

The only reaction to her words was another pull at the whiskey, and a shrug before he left the kitchen.

Henry Newcastle and Mrs. Austen were the first to turn in for the night. From there, it was Samantha and Charles who departed. Soon, George found himself left with the same party as he had had at the piano bar those months back, plus Chelsea.

The blonde had remembered her sweater when she came back out, but it didn't stop her from sitting far closer to George than he liked for warmth. It was a minor annoyance, but when you had Paulo in the room to contrast it with, minor annoyances became trivial.

Although his drink had long since been exhausted, George didn't get back up for another. Instead, he suffered listening to Paulo and occasionally getting in a few words himself. Chelsea ventured a question, and once a comment, to which Paulo gave his indescribable charm and attention, leaving the girl feeling like her question went unanswered and her comment unheard.

Margaret alone in the group appeared to have actual interest in what Paulo had to say, nodding attentively, even prodding him along at various points when George would have rather prodded him into the lake with a pair of cement shoes on his feet.

"I'm calling it a night," Margaret announced eventually.

"I should too," George agreed, yawning. If he struggled to sleep tonight, he couldn't blame Paulo.

Chelsea, whose drowsiness was more than apparent, seconded the yawn.

The party ascended the staircase and made their way to their rooms. George had purposefully picked the one closest to the upstairs library. At first he was taken aback when Chelsea was following him, only to discover she had taken the room directly adjacent to his.

"Good night," she said with a small wave. "See you tomorrow."

"See you tomorrow," George agreed. Glancing down the hallway he could see Margaret quickly turn from looking at them and retreat into her own room.

Dropping onto the bed, he sighed. This vacation was already becoming more complicated than he had anticipated. Now he had two factors he hadn't prepared for: Margaret Clarke and Paulo Castillo. He had prepared to deal with Helen, he had made peace with having to endure Charles's company, but these were not variables he had any sense of readiness for. Not that it mattered. There was no bad blood between him and Margaret now; she hadn't even tried to rattle him about his book. Paulo might be a bore, but bores could be endured; after all, Charles was already here.

Slowly, George stretched his neck, rotating it clockwise, hoping to loosen the tension which was already building. Yes, he would survive, but maybe he was looking at this wrong anyway. Survival was the minimum. Why not try to use the situation to his advantage? Now, there were people in play he hadn't planned for, which allowed him a wider range of options and opportunities than he had initially hoped for. Adding Margaret to the mix came with challenges, but also with opportunities which were not entirely unpleasant to imagine. As the plans began to form in his head, each iteration was tested for strength and endurance before it was discarded for a better one. George relaxed on the bed and closed his eyes.

CHAPTER 14

Knowing everyone else would sleep late, George rose early purposefully. Stealing softly down the stairs, he made it safely to the kitchen and the coffee maker. He tried to keep things as quiet as he could to preserve the few moments of solitude he could count on in the early hours of the morning.

Scrambling his eggs and sipping his coffee, George enjoyed the smug feeling of superiority all early risers do when comparing themselves to their slumbering counterparts. Dropping the eggs onto his plate, wisps of steam rising from the small stack, he was about to go sit on the patio to enjoy the morning sunrise with his breakfast when he was arrested by seeing someone else already there. Through the window he spotted Margaret, mug in hand, watching the dawn. As the sun rose, it caused her hair to shine and her face to smile. There was no reason he couldn't or shouldn't join her, but before she could catch sight of him, George retreated back to the dining room away from view. He excused himself by insisting it was to preserve his morning solitude.

Between bites of breakfast, George wrote idly in his commonplace book. Much like his morning pages, these lines were unrestricted and uncensored; whatever he thought was set on the page in a coherent or incoherent way. Like a piano player stretching their fingers with scales, this was how he tried to keep his mind limber for the harder work ahead.

The promise of dawn illuminated another day by the lake. Dew glistened in the yards and the lake glittered. In spite of the summer, the morning was still cool enough for steam to rise off the mug of coffee, hovering like the mists which would evaporate off the lake before her. Quietly, she enjoyed the first sip of morning brew while gazing at the beauty of everything around her, even as everything around her gazed at the beauty of her...

George stopped writing. This was rubbish, even for the idle moments of morning. He was about to violently cross out his scribbles when he heard the sliding door open—Margaret coming back inside, no doubt. Instead of greeting her, he abandoned his dishes on the table where they lay. A plate with a few scrambled eggs on it was not an unfamiliar sight to Samantha, who would know it was George's and take it away when she discovered it.

Hours later, as the rest of the house woke up and started milling about, George was in the library. He had his laptop queued to his notes for *Until All Graces*. Serenity was here, a peace which came from having all he needed to do what he wanted. A knock came from the door. It was his mother who entered.

"We're getting ready to go to town," she said.

"Fantastic, have a great time," he replied without looking up from the screen.

"Don't you want to come with?"

"No," he said, looking up. "I want to use the time you're gone to write in peace."

"You could have done that at home."

"I want to do it here too."

His mother shrugged and left him to his pages.

A minute passed before George was interrupted again, barely making it past the first page. This time it was Chelsea. "You aren't coming to town?" she asked.

"No. You'll have a great time though, Mother knows where everything is."

"Well, if you're staying I might as well too," she decided—irrationally, George thought.

Chelsea left, leaving George in peace again. He made it down the second page before he was interrupted a third time, and this the least pleasant so far. It was Paulo.

"George!" he proclaimed, waddling into the library and taking a seat beside George.

"Yes?" George ventured cautiously.

"I had planned on going to town to see the sights today. However, since Margaret Clarke has decided to stay, I too have decided to stay. There will be other days I can go when we all can make the visit. It is beautiful here. Besides, I'll have a great time discussing literature with you."

Looking up from his laptop screen, George debated if the lifetime in prison for manslaughter was worth the afternoon speaking with Paulo about literature. He decided it wasn't.

Chelsea returned to the library. Looking around the room, books across every wall, she idly picked a volume of love poetry. Lounging on the couch across from George, she began to page through it. Every now and again she'd interrupt Paulo's stream of words pouring at George with her thoughts about the poems or reading lines aloud. This was not a situation he could endure for long.

"Excuse me," George said, closing the laptop and tucking it under his arm as he rose, "I need to get my charger."

He found his charger, and then his car.

Boxed and Burlap was a local coffee chain with a couple of locations around the lake. George's chosen retreat was the original one built on the corner of two highways, just outside of Williams Bay.

He made his order at the front of the shop, a caramel macchiato, a drink he only ever ordered at this shop because they made it differently. It tasted better than the one time he had asked Josiah to make it for him back home. The shop was surprisingly slow for a Friday morning, but he didn't complain. It meant he had his pick of places to sit.

George elected to occupy one of the four large chairs which took the center of the main room. Sometimes when he was there, he would hide in the loft, enjoying the marginally higher volume of solitude he could gain there. Right now, he actually was in the mood to people watch between paragraphs.

"Caramel macchiato!" the barista declared, and George waited a moment before he remembered his coffee wouldn't be delivered to him here. The price one paid for being on vacation. As he grabbed his coffee, he glanced at the sign which hung at the side exit. It was one of the reasons he first liked the shop. The sign read "The Man in the Arena" and gave the final paragraph of Theodore Roosevelt's "Citizenship in a Republic" speech. "Whose place shall never be with those cold and timid souls who know neither victory, nor defeat," George said quietly under his breath. A good reminder, and a better use of wall space than he's seen in most coffee shops.

Settling into the large armchair, coffee lazily hanging from the fingers of his right hand while he scrolled the pages of *Until All Graces* with the left, George fell into a routine. He would review a page, then look up and see who was here. Paraded past him was a revolving circle of soccer moms, business people running in and out, a couple of wedding coordinators speaking to enthusiastic (if delusional) young couples. Maybe there was a sense of moral superiority he felt, a delight in the general lack of responsibility he had compared to those around him. Why not choose to enjoy it? Hadn't he earned it?

Compared to the bustle he had begun to feel in the lake house, the rotation of customers in and out of the shop was a reprieve. Everyone had a different version of relaxing, but it shocked George how many other people found he was required for them to accomplish it. Which was one of the reasons he had been prudent enough to drive his own vehicle here in the first place. Certainly, he acted like the world revolved around him, but he didn't intend anyone else to take it seriously. To prevent the potential for people trying to locate him, George had turned off his phone. This prevented him from using the maps function, but of the only three places in the area he knew how to drive to without directions, Boxed and Burlap was the only one he needed today.

Between scrolling through the pages, sipping coffee, and people watching, George found himself thinking about the people he had abandoned in the house. There still wasn't a satisfactory answer for why Paulo was there at all, and of course the eternal question of what to do about Charles. There he thought he might have an idea. Crazy though it might be, it could work if he could get the help he needed. He had avoided Margaret this morning and, try as he might, there wasn't a rational answer he could muster for it. Eventually he'd find one. After all, he did nothing without a rational motivation.

There was a relaxing summer breeze passing through the open windows. It almost made George want to move outside to the patio seating. Before he could make the choice, casually looking around the room, his eyes fixed on her. Standing there at the edge of the bar, waiting for her coffee, she had on a summer dress that was admittedly eye catching and a short khaki hat. He could run again, retreat upstairs in hopes she didn't catch his movement. He could take the initiative and go up and say hi. He could simply remain where he was seated and wait for her to see him and make up her own mind. The last idea came with both the least amount of movement and effort on his part, so he remained. There was always a chance she didn't notice he was there.

"Hi George." She waved.

Seating herself in the armchair across from George, Margaret Clarke set her small stack of books on the little coffee table between them. There was a novel of some kind she was reading, along with two notebooks.

"Nice place," Margaret commented, sipping on her coffee.

"It's a good place to hide," George admitted.

"Well, is that what you're doing here, hiding?" she asked, stretching into a yawn.

"Technically, I'm working." George specified, indicating the computer on his lap.

"On the novel you're denying me a sneak peek of?" she asked, with a smile.

"Precisely."

"So my best plan is to quickly read as much as I can the next time you step into the bathroom?"

George laughed, but, he also found himself starting to think about the bathroom. She probably wasn't joking, either.

"What do you think of the lake so far?" George asked politely.

Margaret's eyes roamed the room. "I haven't seen much yet," she decided, "but what I've seen, I've liked."

"You should have gone with the group this morning," George said. "You could have gotten a great tour from Henry Newcastle. Helen could have shown you every spot in the town where you can make a child cry."

"Maybe next time," she decided, drinking her coffee with a smirk.

"Why don't I take you on the nickel tour?" he offered. "I'm just about done here anyway."

Margaret looked around the room until her attention became fixed on something in the other room. "First, a game of chess," she decided. "Winner pays the nickel."

George cocked an eyebrow. "Are you sure?"

"Unless you're chicken."

"Not at all, I just hate to take advantage of people."

"I'm not entirely sure I believe that. Besides, you'll have to prove it."

Each took a different side of the oversized chess board. Each piece on the board was the size of their coffee cups. George gave her the benefit of playing as white, and he made the decision not to stretch himself—just let the game unfold. Chess, as a game, was simple in nature. Any complexity was added by people who hadn't studied it. Victory inevitably fell to the person who knew what they were doing.

As they began to play, George realized Margaret wasn't as bad at the game as he expected, though she wasn't particularly good at it either. They each made their opening moves. George had his strategy somewhat made in advance, taking an opening formation which usually served him well. Margaret deliberated over every move, considering all the angles. George didn't waste time reassessing what he already knew, that he was going to win. She didn't make it as easy as he had expected, though. Each time he was about to close in for the kill, she'd slip away like a desert mirage.

"Finally," he said, close to exasperation when the white king was set into checkmate.

"Fine," Margaret huffed, knocking the king over as delicately as a French mob.

"Poor sportsmanship doesn't become anyone," George chided teasingly. "If you can't lose, you can't play."

"Is that why you're dating Chelsea?" she asked sharply.

The question took George off guard. "What are you implying?"

"Chelsea is easy, and you don't take risks," she spat.

Narrowing his eyebrows, George said, with gravel in his voice. "As I apparently need to clarify to everyone, Chelsea and I are not dating. She's just a friend."

"Does she know that?" Margaret asked pointedly. "With how cozy the two of you were last night, I don't think so."

"Of course," George said. "She's just an affectionate person."

The scorn on Margaret's face didn't do much to hide what she thought of that statement. "I read people," she stated. "That's not what Chelsea's appearance was saying."

He wanted to defend his reasoning, but he didn't have to read people to know her expression meant she wasn't about to be swayed. Instead, he asked, "Do you still want the tour? Forget the nickel, it's on the house." He smiled.

It wasn't often Margaret had seen George give a true, honest grin, one which didn't read with the pinch marks of forcing it. Not everyone would have noticed the difference between his real smile and the fake one, but she could.

"Alright," she acquiesced. "Show me around here."

George did. He took her first to Yerkes Observatory, home to the world's largest refracting telescope. They drove down the hill, through the small village of Williams Bay and up another hill to where the large dome sat dominating the landscape of trees and yards. He didn't know why they built the telescope here, but it was a feature and an oddity which proved how random life could become.

After that, they drove to Lake Geneva proper. The downtown district was busy, as always. They drove round, and round, and round a couple of blocks looking for parking.

"I didn't know so much of the tour involved crawling past occupied parking," Margaret teased.

"It's one of the biggest attractions," George quipped.

Eventually, they found a spot on the far side of town near the building called the Horticultural Hall. The benefit was, it did allow them to walk past most of the town to get to the lake.

It was easy to forget how beautiful the lake was, George thought. Looking around from the Riveria building, he was astonished at how crystal the water looked, the dazzling nature of sunlight and water mixing to create a dancing mirror that erupted in small waves every time a boat passed.

They walked to the library park and took a bench. He couldn't hold back any longer, he had to ask her, and there was no better time than now. "Margaret, I have a question I've been meaning to ask you," he began cautiously.

"Yes?" she asked, a little breathless and a little hopeful.

He paused to take a deep breath. "Will you seduce Charles for me?"

CHAPTER 15

"You want me to *what*?!" Margaret demanded. "No!"

"Just get him to kiss you or something," George insisted. "Not sleep with him or anything drastic."

"Still no!" Margaret shouted, leaping off the bench. "Why would you ask me that?"

"Well, I could have asked Helen, but I can't see her convincingly seducing anyone," he explained calmly.

"That's a horrible plan," Margaret declared. "I can't believe you asked me that."

"It's the last thing I can think of," George said. "If you could compromise him, then I can show Samantha the kind of person he is."

"He's annoying, but he's not a cheater."

"I've tried to break them up twice already. Neither option worked. This is the only thing I can think of. I thought you'd be on board."

Margaret sighed and rubbed her temples. "No, a million times no. George, I might have helped if you asked me to do anything else, but not this, definitely not this."

"Well, how do you suggest I break them up then?" he asked irritably.

"I don't think you need to. Charles is annoying, but who cares. If Samantha doesn't mind, it's not your business."

"She's my sister. She doesn't know what kind of mistake he is. I know better."

"And she can make her own choices," Margaret reminded him. "Hard as this is to imagine, you don't always know better."

George grit his teeth. He wasn't in the mood to defend himself. "Of course I do!" he insisted. "I'm older, wiser, and more successful."

"Which still doesn't mean you know better," she reiterated. "If you've told her you don't like him, you've done your part. Let her live her life. You're also the person who just asked a girl to seduce a guy he doesn't like, does that sound like the plan of someone who knows better?" She crossed her arms, disappointed. "You're afraid of losing your sister, and you're doing everything you can to stop that from happening. You've been so frightened of him taking away your sister, all you can do is see the parts you don't like. Have you asked yourself if you might be overreacting?"

He gave her a freezing glare that actually caused her to shudder as if a cold wind blew past. "You aren't going to help," he said flatly.

"No, I'm not. I'm actually hurt you even asked me to help you like this," she said, a sullen note in her voice.

The two were now both standing. A brief memory passed through George's mind of another couple once happy and smiling turn to yelling and screaming at one another in a park. Now, he was no longer a spectator, but a participant.

"Please take me back," Margaret said quietly.

Before they could leave, they were halted by Henry Newcastle calling them.

It was with a mixture of relief and frustration George and Margaret were adopted into the Newcastle party. His mother hadn't seemed to notice any of the drama which had recently unfolded. George thought Helen appeared to pick up on something, but she said nothing about it. Samantha and Charles were there, walking arm and arm. They didn't have eyes for anyone but each other. Henry Newcastle was enthusiastically sharing the history of the library park with Margaret, and George debated how long to stay.

Consciously or unconsciously, the two drifted to opposite sides of the party. Margaret at the head of the group, learning more than she anticipated about the history of the lake and its culture, while George retreated to the back. Helen drifted beside him and gave him a look. "So, where have you two been?" she asked conspiratorially.

"I was just giving her a tour," he said icily, keeping back the irritation which still dwelt in his mind. No matter how sour he might feel, there was no value in showing it, especially to Helen.

She murmured an acknowledgement, but didn't venture any further questions.

The party walked around the shops, with Mrs. Austen giving her commentary about where was worth buying from and not. She added anecdotes about shops or storefronts she had remembered being there in the past but hadn't survived to today. George heard none of it, allowing everything said to drift past him like rednecks down a lazy river. His mind was turned to the question of his mission to get rid of Charles. Perhaps seduction was an extreme measure after all. Was he really going to be so readily pushed to it? Maybe he'd get lucky and while they were walking down the road a car would hop the curb and crush Charles. Tragedy or miracle, it would depend on who you asked. He tried to look at the matter rationally. If he had truly taken every measure within his power, it should be the end of it, and maybe there was some shred of truth in him being worried about losing his sister.

When Mrs. Austen had exhausted her words on the topic of the Lake Geneva downtown district, Henry Newcastle suggested they return to the house for lunch and a few rounds on the boat. Margaret said she'd ride back with everyone else, leaving George on his own. Once alone, he allowed the storm clouds gathered above his head to obscure the sunshine of the day. He let loose a few four-letter thunderbolts from between his lips as he stalked back to his car. He didn't have time to worry about this, he had a party to prepare for.

CHAPTER 16

"I want to know about Cynthia," Margaret announced.

Helen looked up from her book. After getting back from their Lake Geneva tour, the two had settled back into their rooms theoretically to prepare for the night's party, but Helen had found a book at a local bookstore while they were walking and immediately settled to browse through it. Margaret had been pacing back and forth. She occasionally had settled into scrolling on her phone, until it displeased her and she went back to pacing. Helen didn't care; the carpet in the room needed replacing anyway.

Finally, Margaret asked the question which had been on her mind ever since she'd last overheard the name which was always met with a shush. "Who was Cynthia?" she reiterated.

Sighing, Helen closed her book. Pursing her lips, she thought back to where it had started. Back to when George didn't openly flinch at hearing the word "romance."

"She was the artist who designed the cover art for George's first book, and she became a friend," Helen explained.

"And she became more than friends with George?" Margaret pressed.

Helen nodded. "They did…" She tapered off, trying to find the precise way of expressing what hell it had been for all of them. Watching George wither with Cynthia. They had thought it would bring ruin to his career. "They became more than friends, after George practically went to the ends of the earth for her."

Margaret cocked an eyebrow. "George was a romantic?"

"Back then, he was. He did everything he could to win Cynthia's heart, and they dated, but he was always more invested in the relationship than she was. As such things go, they broke up. George was left with his heart in tatters and she walked away with nary a scratch."

"She sounds like a horrible person," Margaret said empathetically.

"Cynthia was just a person as selfish as the rest of us," Helen corrected. "They were never a well-matched couple from the start. George's all single-malt scotch and pressed suits, while she thought wearing anything other than sweatpants and a sweatshirt was classing it up."

Margaret laughed. "She doesn't sound like George's kind of girl."

"She was in only one respect—she had a witty sense of humor. The two of them bantered like Olympic fencers."

"Like the two of you," Margaret pointed out, giving Helen a meaningful look.

"No, no. No. No," Helen insisted with a laugh.

"Never?" Margaret asked, eyebrow cocked. "The two of you have known each other since childhood. Hard to imagine you never went on a single date."

"I'd like to think he had a crush on me when we were kids, but short of going through his teenage journals I'll never know," Helen admitted. "And going out with him just to see the mortification on his mother's face would almost make it worth it, but any chance we might have had is long gone."

Serious, Margaret asked, "Do you wish it hadn't?"

"On paper, you might think George and I would make a good match," Helen answered, "but in reality we're too alike. We'd constantly be fighting to see who was the superior being and it would get old faster than we would."

Accepting the answer, Margaret nodded thoughtfully. She was still reeling over what George had asked her in the park, and what she had hoped he would have asked her instead.

CHAPTER 17

Life is a performance, and some are better actors than others. It doesn't matter if it's a quiet conversation between lovers in cafe, the bombastic entrance before a rapturous crowd of admirers, or any of the many scenes of life in between. Most people are consumed with how well they are performing, how well their lines are being received by the audience, real or imagined. The remarkable ones are the naturals, who walk across the stages of life without noticing the audience, cameras, or script. They know the role they are there to play and play it without a second thought.

Scale doesn't matter. However large or small the scene, it only elevates or compresses the dramatic tension of the occasion. At the birthday party of Henry Newcastle, there was no one who wasn't preparing for a performance, consciously or not. With each look in the mirror, adjustment of a tie or evening gown, the guests were preparing for their roles. Tonight, the scale would be large, the set enormous, and the drama palpable. It would be a night where life elevated beyond the conventional narrative and tilted ever so slightly into a heightened reality. Where the lines between story and life would blur in the most exciting ways. Guests would leave with a memory they could cherish for a lifetime, the heady delight of the first glass of champagne drawn out through an entire evening.

Everything about black tie events appealed to George. Everything except the black tie. For more than half an hour, George had been in front of the mirror of his room trying to solve the complicated puzzle that was the bow tie. He could have purchased the kind which was pre-tied. It could have been clipped into place within a minute with no effort. Had he done that, George wouldn't have been able to look himself in the mirror. Anything worth doing was worth doing right, which was why he was literally twisting himself in knots over it. However rough he thought he had it, George knew he didn't want to begin considering what dark magic was being worked by the girls in their rooms to prepare for tonight.

It would be a night to remember, George knew it in the bones of his fingers. A Newcastle birthday party was an event which drew the literati from various corners of the globe. While considered a successful author, George was a flash in the pan in comparison to the pantheon of experience and authorial gravity which would be present tonight. Even if his title was only "editor," Henry Newcastle's reputation and influence was wide and vast. He had worked with some of the most interesting writers of the age, and they wanted to be there to celebrate his birthday.

Having done his homework, George knew who he was there to talk to tonight. Usually, he would have gone over his game plan with Samantha in advance, so she could provide whatever support was needed. Yesterday, when had tried discussing it with her, she was distracted and disinterested. More invested in Charles having a good time tonight than George having a successful one. Unconsciously, the thought made George clench his jaw.

Gaining victory over the bowtie, George gave himself a final inspection. Approving of the reflection, he left to join the festivities. Arriving at the bottom of the staircase in the hall, George straightened his shirt cuffs and took stock of the room. The dinner party he had hosted was nothing compared to tonight. The comparison would be like cat and a lion—both were felines, but there the similarities ended. He had heard Henry say there were over three hundred on the guest list, with expectations of another hundred to show up uninvited. Some would be neighbors from around the lake and community, others would be the plus-sevens invited by other guests. It didn't matter to Henry. For as long as George had known him, the large and outlandish birthday party was an event which Henry wanted to share with anyone. Anyone including Paulo, apparently.

Out of the corner of his eye, George could see the literature professor passing through guests headed his direction. George pretended not to notice and looked for the nearest exit. Ducking out to the patio, he plucked a flute of champagne off a passing waiter's tray. Looking around, he appreciated the detail that had been taken in setting the stage for the night. Within hours of the event company arriving, the house, already stately, became a palace from a storybook. George was too rational to fall in love with the story their world would fall into for the night, but he knew the power it would hold over almost everyone else there.

Glancing around quickly to ensure he was safe, George strode out towards the band. He hadn't seen his family yet, or the

Newcastles, but there would be ample time in the evening for them. At the other end of the patio, near the brass band, George could see Anthony Stapleton and his wife Katherine.

Approaching, the friends greeted one another warmly, while Katherine satisfied herself with a look of acknowledgement.

"Are we sure Henry isn't Jay Gatsby in disguise?" Anthony asked humorously.

"You're the spy, you tell me," George replied.

"Case officer," Anthony corrected. Changing the subject, he asked, "How are things with Chelsea?"

George shrugged. "Fine. I've finished the first draft, she came to Lake Geneva as a thank-you from me for the help."

Nodding with a knowing look, Anthony said roguishly, "To thank her, I'm sure."

"You know I'm not like that," George replied, drinking his champagne.

"Warm-blooded? Heaven forbid," Anthony mocked.

Before he had a chance to give Anthony a withering stare, they were interrupted by Chelsea herself. Having caught sight of George, she took a position by his side. As beautiful as ever, she was dressed in a shimmering black evening gown that highlighted the best of her figure and features.

Politely, George introduced Chelsea to the Stapletons. After the introduction, Anthony gave George an approving look his friend ignored.

"George has been telling us how you've been an asset in developing his next book," Anthony remarked.

"It's been fun to be a part of the process," Chelsea bubbled. "I love to see how he takes something I say and turns it into a story."

"Yes," Anthony muttered. "The charm of that eventually wears off."

"Hey," George interrupted, "you should know better than to assume anything you say won't be used somehow in a story."

"I do now," Anthony said resignedly.

"After he had to explain why a realistic description of a particular facility in a particular country showed up in a novel to his boss," Katherine added coldly.

"It worked out," Anthony said hastily, cutting off whatever other thoughts his wife might have added to George's writing.

As much fun as catching up with his friends was, George was not there to see them but the wider circle of acquaintances that he either already had or were yet to be made. Offering Chelsea his arm, he wished his friends a pleasant evening, and made his way into the sea of people.

There was no doubt, having Chelsea at his arm enhanced George's presence as he glad-handed. At first, he was unsure how to introduce her, but quickly discovered no one asked. Probably they assumed, but he didn't care about their assumptions. He was there to meet and impress his peers.

There was a Western novelist he was happy to become reacquainted with, and they had a brief aside about the fate of the genre in a world becoming more removed from that period of history. He had a delightful conversation with a Hollywood screenwriter who was known for action comedies. They each shared their favorite one-liners and debated what made one good, bad, or so bad it was good. He met with a thriller writer he had crossed paths with a dozen times, but never had a chance to really meet. The more he talked, the more momentum he was gaining. Moving from person to person, topic to topic, George was proving just how much he could work a crowd if he was interested in it. His velocity came to an abrupt halt when he caught sight of *her* from across the patio. Unconsciously, he took in a sharp breath. Diverting his gaze, he resumed his energetic conversation about Fleming versus le Carré.

Eventually, George and Chelsea found themselves with Charles and Samantha, who were with the Stapletons.

"Bag your white whale?" Samantha asked George.

"My harpoon remains in the boat." George sighed. "So far Senator G— has yet to be seen." He glanced around, on the chance saying the name of his quarry aloud would manifest him nearby.

"The two of you make a gorgeous couple," Charles interjected.

George ignored the comment, but Chelsea replied, "Thanks," without correcting her brother.

Anthony gave George a mischievous smile as he drank more champagne, but said nothing. Like the best of friends, he knew when a look would say more than any words.

"Let's dance," Chelsea said to George.

The request bounced off the first time, as he was consumed with watching the party around them, but when she proposed it a second time he caught the message. It might have been her sudden pinch on his upper arm which broke through.

The rest of the company watched as George led Chelsea to the dance floor. Each had their own view of what was going on, but none speculated aloud.

"Do you think Cynthia is coming?" Anthony asked absently, to no one in particular.

Whirling like mongoose after a cobra, Samantha turned on Anthony, shushing him.

"George can't hear me from here," he defended himself with a shrug.

"We aren't taking that chance," Samantha insisted, emphasizing with a poke of her index finger.

The mechanics of dancing were muscle memory to George. The lessons had drilled into his memory and synapses for the right steps at the right times, but his attention wasn't on his steps, the music, or the girl in his arms. His thoughts circled through the mental list of people he still wanted to speak with before the night ended.

"You'll miss a step," Chelsea warned quietly into his ear.

"I haven't missed a step in years," George replied defensively. Whether he was referring to the dance floor or his life was up for debate.

The two danced three songs, and George was delighted to see Henry Newcastle watching, with Senator G—.

"Let's wish Henry a happy birthday," he suggested.

"I'm going to refresh my drink and chat with Charles and Samantha," Chelsea said. "Enjoy talking to the senator," she added with a wink.

Henry wasn't surprised to see George appear as he was speaking to the senator. It freed him from needing to seek him out from the crowd.

"Senator, allow me to introduce one of my finest authors, and something of a protégé. George Austen," Henry said.

"Mr. Austen," the senator said, taking the extended hand, "Henry has been telling me a lot about your talent for dramatizing politics."

"The drama is already there, I just exploit it," George said humbly. He was about to add his thoughts to the senator's particular story when Henry cleared his throat.

"Senator, I'd also like to introduce to you another young author I've been honored to publish. Ms. Margaret Clarke, she wrote—"

"*Good Intentions!*" the senator interrupted. "My wife and I loved your book and enjoyed every word."

George had known he couldn't avoid her the entire night, but from the time he had seen her across the party, he knew he would have to try. Margaret Clarke was breathtaking tonight, in the most literal sense. Wearing a lake-blue evening gown which highlighted the best of her figure, her hair worn high with golden ringlets framing her face, she looked like a princess from a fairytale.

"Thank you," Margaret replied, giving the senator a small curtsey. "It's nice to know some people don't judge books by their genres," she added, a verbal swipe at George.

"I actually have a weakness for a good romance," the senator admitted. "It's a bit of an escape from the constant power plays in the political scene."

"Love certainly has enough power dynamics of its own," George observed mildly, restraining any irritability from his voice.

"George Austen!" a woman's voice called from behind.

Turning, George was confronted with a face he vaguely recognized but couldn't place. "Yes?" he asked with confusion.

"It's me," she said, her words slurring with the effect of too much drink. "You haven't returned my phone calls or text messages. It was just one date and then..." As she babbled, George had the dawning realization this was one of the girls he had a dinner date with, and as his mind frantically searched for her name, he remembered she was the one who had a habit of drama and emotional outbursts. His eyes widened. This was far from ideal.

"Isabelle!" Samantha called, catching the girl's attention. "Hey girl, I have to introduce you to this cute guy I met."

"Really?" Isabelle asked, sufficiently distracted to follow Samantha. As she led the girl away, the sister glanced at George with a wry smile.

"I apologize for the interruption," George said to the senator. "There was a misunderstanding."

"What I was your age I had a few 'misunderstandings' with women myself," the senator said reassuringly.

"No, no," George tried to explain, "it's not like that."

"It's exactly like that," Margaret corrected amusedly.

"I have to add, the two of you make a handsome couple," the senator complimented.

The two authors suddenly realized they had drifted next to one another, standing close enough to feel the warmth of the other. Instantly, they stepped apart.

"We're not a couple," George scoffed.

"Not in the slightest," Margaret added hastily.

The senator shrugged. "My mistake. Politics makes you see all sorts of things which aren't really there."

He asked George what he thought about how to tell his story as a memoir. Excitedly, the author offered his idea of how to frame the senator's story in such a way to highlight his political career and platform. After listening attentively, the senator thanked George for his thoughts and excused himself to mingle with the other guests.

Pleased, George was about to share his thoughts on the interaction with Margaret, only to discover she'd vanished. Instead, Chelsea had materialized by his side, offering him a full flute of champagne.

"Salut," George toasted, and took a long pull of his drink.

It was not long before George found himself standing beside Helen Newcastle. Charles, Samantha, and Margaret were chatting freely, while the two rationalists stood idly by. Neither listened to the conversation, but began watching the party beyond them. For all the competition and challenge they gave each other, they respected that they both saw the world the same way.

Catching Helen looking at him with an amused grin, he quietly asked, "Did you poison my champagne?"

"It's only entertaining if you can solve the problem, or squirm. Poison accomplishes neither."

"Why the amusement then?"

"It's nothing... I simply know something you don't."

"Doubtful."

Looking at George's piercing blue eyes, Helen wondered if he had any idea what she was talking about. He was as quick as her, but this was the black hole of his world, the one area he would avoid at all cost. As tempting as it would be to use this against him, here was where she would draw the line.

"You and Margaret haven't said much to each other tonight," Helen noted, a hint of curiosity shading her voice.

If she was hoping to see George stiffen or flinch, she was disappointed. Calmly, he replied, "Really?" and drank more champagne.

"Oh my god," Helen breathed, he eyes drawn away from George. She had almost pushed the issue, but was shocked by the sight of Paulo approaching the group. The English professor was wearing a long tailcoat, with tails actually trailing behind him on the ground like a bridal train. Across his rounded chest, he had fastened a red sash, like a beauty queen announcing her state of residence. "I can't believe he didn't wear medals too," Helen gasped with a laugh.

"If he had them, he would," George replied seriously.

"He could have his own made."

"Don't mention that," George warned. "He'll tell us about what he'll reward himself for, and I'm not drunk enough to find that enjoyable."

"You should learn to be more amused by the mortals," Helen chided. "Otherwise you'll grouse."

"Because you're such a ray of sunshine and everyone loves how you treat them?" George replied sarcastically.

In thought, Helen tapped her champagne flute with a fingertip. "It's not that I'm any more likable than you are, I just accept I don't care whether they do or don't."

"I don't care," George said defensively, crossing his arms.

Helen laughed. "Oh, you do, more than you ever want to admit or consider. You want the attention and adoration. Which is why you don't like Charles."

"What does this have to do with Charles?" George growled.

"He's likable, even if he's uninteresting and mundane," she reasoned, "I don't need to have Margaret's eyes to see you're jealous of how he has Samantha's attention. Attention which, until recently, was devoted and undivided toward you."

Before he could argue his point, they were interrupted by the fullness of Paulo's presence. He gave a courtly bow to them before directing his attention to Margaret, who had been speaking in hushed tones with Samantha.

"Ms. Clarke, will you do me the honor of joining me in a dance?" he entreated, with a deeper bow.

As Margaret searched for an excuse, Helen stepped in. "She's already promised to dance with George for the next four dances," she supplied with a smile.

Paulo did a poor job of hiding his disappointment, while Margaret shot a glare Helen's direction.

Without skipping a beat, George extended his hand to Margaret. She accepted it graciously, although he couldn't gauge whether she was irritated with Helen for suggesting it or him for playing along. As they left for the dance floor, she stopped, turned to Paulo, and said, "I'm sure Helen would be delighted to dance with you." Turning on her heel, she left Helen to Paulo's charms.

A schoolboy smirk played at the edges of George's face as they started to dance. Margaret was stiff and detailed, going through each step mechanically, as if deaf to the music crooning behind her. Her disinterest was annoying him more than he expected.

"If you don't want to be here, you don't have to be. I was trying to help," George found himself muttering.

He could see her jaw clench as she considered a reply, but she bit it back, for some reason he couldn't discern. George didn't like to waste time; this was his way of being a friend. If she didn't care, he certainly didn't feel obligated to do so either.

Without warning, he felt her relax in his arms. The stiffness and chill of the moment melted like the frost before the morning dawn. She leaned into him as they moved across the dance floor, still silent, but no longer defensive. Stepping in rhythm with the music, they were close enough he could feel the beat of her heart. For a moment, their eyes met. His as blue as the dress she was wearing, hers as warm as a winter flame. The spell broke as the music ended, and each stepped back, wary and distant.

"Thank you for dancing," Margaret said hurriedly and disappeared into the crowd, leaving George without another word.

Like a fading spell, George could feel the energy that had carried him through the night ebbing away. He had expended vastly more social currency than usual, and as the drain set in, he found a quiet chair near the bar to relax in. He wasn't alone for long, but it was long enough he didn't quite growl when Samantha, Charles, Chelsea, and Helen found him. Lazily, he only glanced to acknowledge their existence and returned to scratching his pen on the napkin in front of him.

"Successful night?" Chelsea asked, taking the chair next to him.

"Generally," he decided with a sigh.

"Don't sound so disappointed," Helen teased. "You've won the senator's affections, and I've overheard at least a dozen people saying you're going to be the next Fitzgerald."

"Hopefully minus the alcoholism and early death," George retorted.

"Don't worry, you're already a borderline alcoholic," Samantha chimed in. "You don't want to see how much we spend on scotch a month," she added to Charles.

After giving his sister a quick glare, George returned to his scribbles.

"What are you writing?" Chelsea asked, looking at the napkin.

An excellent question, what had he written? They were merely sketches of his mind, unconsciously dropped onto the nearest available canvas. Experience had taught him tablecloths were harder to take away if he had written something worthwhile, so he picked up a couple of napkins and began scratching out a handful of sentences. Reading them for the first time, he was surprised to see their content.

"Nothing," he said hurriedly, tearing the napkin in two. "Just scribbles."

Paulo wandered over to the group, a bead of sweat dropping down his forehead as he collapsed onto a chair. "It has been an exhausting evening," he said, taking one of the discarded scraps of the napkin George had dropped to dab at his forehead.

Anthony and Katherine Stapleton passed by with Margaret Clarke. The girls were giggling to one another, and Anthony said something that brought their giggles to a boil of laughter. "Well, George, we're taking off," his friend announced, giving George a half-hug.

"You aren't staying the night?" George asked, surprised. He knew there were ample rooms available and expected for use that night.

"I want to get home to my own bed," Anthony admitted, "and since Katherine's game for an evening drive home, we're taking our chances."

"Katherine," George acknowledged with civility.

"George," she replied in kind. "It was good to see you again," she added more warmly to Margaret.

After waving a final goodbye, Margaret took a seat next to Helen. Her eyes flashed at George and darted away before he could meet her gaze.

"George has a protégé at the coffee shop back home," Chelsea remarked.

"Really?" Samantha asked incredulously. "Some young blonde with mooning eyes hanging on to his every word?"

"Josiah isn't blonde," George answered quietly with a smirk. "He needed some advice and I offered the best I could."

"*Romantic* advice," Chelsea added with amusement, squeezing George's shoulder.

"You?" Margaret asked, her voice more incredulous than she had expected it to be.

"What did you tell him?" Samantha asked.

"Wait, I know," Helen proposed with a wry smile. "He said love is a fleeting emotion and as a teenager he shouldn't expect any relationship formed now to last longer than a bag of roasted coffee. Am I right?"

"Not quite," George corrected. "I told him to manage his expectations and to tell her how he feels."

"Surprisingly sound advice," Samantha said, with Charles even nodding in agreement.

"Even if hypocritical," Margaret added quietly, crossing her arms uncomfortably.

"It was an amazing party tonight," Samantha began, trying to refocus the conversation.

"It was," George agreed. "Margaret, would care to elaborate that thought?"

"You avoid talking about how you feel," Margaret explained coolly. Turning to Chelsea, she asked, "Has he ever talked to you about anything other than what was on his mind?"

Chelsea didn't respond, but glanced at George with a wan smile. Clenching his jaw, George deliberated saying exactly what was on his mind right now.

"Ms. Newcastle, you are a splendid dancer," Paulo interjected. "If only you hadn't twisted your ankle, we could have kept dancing all night long."

Helen, whose ankle was in perfect condition, nodded sadly in agreement.

"Excuse me, I need a drink," George said, rising and buttoning his dinner jacket.

He went to the bar for a glass of champagne, but the bartender was distracted. Rather than wait, he reached around and plucked a bottle of Dom Pérignon from where it was chilling. For a moment, he considered taking it back to the table with him, but why should he? There was nothing to be gained by returning to the rest of the party. Walking off, he popped the cork and filled his glass.

In George's absence, Paulo had taken command of the conversation, discussing the nuances of his narrative and the revenge his protagonist would take on his oppressors. "Like the Count of Monte Cristo?" Helen ventured idly.

"Precisely!" he said, his hand letting go of the tattered napkin George had been writing on.

As the pieces dropped to the table, Margaret could see George's handwriting. Curious, she inconspicuously took the remnants and fit them together to read what had been written. As she finished the words, her cheeks turned rosy. Rising, she excused herself and vanished into the party.

As she left, Helen, who hadn't missed a moment, took up the napkin for herself and read what it said.

Every girl wishes to be the princess at the party, the Cinderella at the ball waiting to meet her Prince Charming. Only one may claim this honor per occasion, but not every one of them meets their prince. Elegant in every way, wearing a dress as blue as heartache, the Cinderella of the evening looked across the room for her prince. Watching her, he hoped for the first time in years. For this princess, he hoped he could be a prince.

Passing through the remains of the party, George looked around at the guests who were still upright and about. The man of the night, Henry Newcastle, had turned in already, and most of the mature adults had followed his example. The night remained to the young and young at heart, who enjoyed the enchantment that remained in the air. Some would call drivers, the more daring would drive themselves, but most would end up spending their night here. Many rooms would be empty, not because they didn't have someone to occupy them, but because guests either didn't make it back to their own rooms or found others' to share.

Arriving at his chosen destination, George stood at the edge of the dock and drank liberally from his glass. The bubbles of the fine champagne served as a tonic to the thoughts he was trying to ignore. Looking out across the lake, he could see the night stars reflected on its surface, dancing like a ballet devoted to praising the sky above.

The lights of each home around the lake glittered, brief specks of self-declaration in the surrounding darkness. Although he didn't spot any green lights off any of the docks, it wasn't hard to think of Jay Gatsby pining after Daisy, watching for the so hued light across from his home. George loved the novel, but he had always been critical of Gatsby's execution on a brilliant plan. The character allowed himself to give up the mystery and illusion too quickly, giving too much of himself to Daisy, a woman who wasn't worth the effort he made. It was the danger of love: It clouded judgement.

Romance, always balanced so delicately between tragedy and comedy. You could never judge appropriately which you lived until the final pages. Even then, it depended where you chose to stop the story.

Stories were the thing George thought he understood best in life. Looking at life dispassionately, he could assess the weaving narratives that made their ways through the day. He could see the differences between the narrative of reality and the narrative desired. Now, he was less certain, more confused. He took another drink, enjoying the numbing effect it had on his ability to think clearly. Counterintuitive though it might be, reducing his ability to think of life clearly seemed the perfect approach in this moment. He had questions, questions he never thought he'd ask himself, but couldn't find answers to them. Life had always been a matter of just living how he wanted and writing what he wanted; now it seemed all so complicated. He took another drink and refilled his empty glass.

If he wanted what he thought he wanted, there would be consequences, there would be dangers, there would be a risk he had sworn he never would take again. He drank again and refilled again. Wrestling inside with the conflict of desire and will, he allowed himself a four-letter oath, spoken aloud to the stars above and the lake below. On the dock he considered the agitation of his heart and drank again. As a violent invective was again about to escape his lips, he was arrested by the sound of footsteps crossing the dock behind him.

CHAPTER 18

"Hey," said a female voice with detached irony, "are you going to fall in?"

"Only if you're going to push me," George replied, as Helen sat down beside him.

"There's no glory in defeating someone who can't defend themselves," she replied matter-of-factly. "How far down the bottle are you, anyway?"

George poured more of the bottle into his glass and took another drink. "Not enough?" he asked, raising his glass in a toast.

"Are you planning on telling me why you're drinking like prohibition starts tomorrow?" Helen asked, arms folded.

"Talking about it changes nothing. So why waste words?"

"Words can't change anything," Helen agreed, tilting her head, "but actions can. In your particular case, I'm afraid yours start with sharing how you feel. There seems to be some tension between you and Margaret. Maybe an argument at the park today?" she prodded.

"What's the point," George stated, taking another drink.

"Did you lose a question mark in your glass?"

"It's a writing theory," he answered slowly. The champagne was affecting his speech, and now he was purposing each word to be as clear as he could form it.

Helen rose, straightened her dress, and said, "Well, you can sit here and espouse your theories with a slur, or you could do what needs to be done. There's a girl inside sick over you, and you're too self-absorbed or afraid to face it."

"Which one?" George asked, taking another healthy swallow.

Helen sighed. "If that's a real question, you're more hopeless than I imagined. Want me to take the bottle before you fall off the dock?"

"No, I think I'll finish it."

Vaguely, George could distinguish the sound of footsteps retreating as he poured another dose of the bubbling liquid into his glass.

"To Henry!" he said in a toast, raising the glass to the lake.

Footsteps pattered again behind him—had Helen decided to take away the champagne by force? George gripped the neck of the bottle unconsciously.

"Hey," Chelsea said, sitting down next to him.

George relaxed his hold on the bottle and set it down on the dock. "Hey," he replied, "I know this sounds crazy, but I've been told we should talk."

"I agree," she said, dipping her big toe into the water.

"You do?" he asked nervously.

She smirked, and leaned next to his ear and blew on it gently.

Surprised, George stiffened involuntarily.

Whispering into his ear, her voice a breathy request: "Come back to my room with me. We can finish celebrating your book together."

Dulled as George's mind was at present, he had a very clear idea how Chelsea wanted to celebrate. She was an exquisitely attractive woman who was suggesting an evening of explicit pleasure. No thinking, just indulgence. Yet, George knew it was never so simple, never so clean as it appeared. In his heart, he wasn't interested in Chelsea, and however attractive she was and however tipsy he was, he wouldn't pretend otherwise.

"No," he said quietly.

Taking him off guard, she leaned in and kissed him passionately. Drawing back with a soft bite on his lips, she asked with a raised eyebrow, "Are you sure?"

He swallowed and refocused, croaking hoarsely, "Yes."

She frowned, obviously not anticipating any resistance on his part.

Before he could do anything about it, George was pushed off the dock and treading water. By the time he pulled himself back up on the wood planks, he was alone again. Well, alone except for the bottle. The glass was gone, probably at the bottom of the lake waiting to be stepped on, so George decided to drink directly from the bottle. He was beyond worrying about tomorrow. Now it was just a matter of finishing what he had started. Seeing a matter to the end was important. It sometimes didn't turn out as planned or projected, and sometimes it just resulted in finishing a bad idea. But he would finish it, holding on until his endurance was completely spent and the project could release him from its grasp. Obsessive madness, hyper-focus, grit, and will—these had carried him through before, and would be the instruments to pull him down to the bottom of this bottle.

Footsteps sounded again. George sincerely hoped it wasn't Chelsea returning to continue her retribution. He held the lip of the dock, which probably wouldn't help at all, but at least it would be resistance of some kind. Besides, it was nice to have some support to keep him from wobbling like a bobber in the lake.

"Hi," said a soft, sweet voice. George looked to see the stars reflected in large brown eyes, their depths mirroring the starlight like the lake around them.

Margaret sat beside George and played with the edge of her dress.

"You're wet," she observed.

"I am," he agreed, removing the dripping bowtie from around his neck.

"Chelsea didn't look happy when she came back inside," Margaret observed.

"Didn't she?" George replied sarcastically, about to drink another pull from the bottle when Margaret took it from him.

He meant to protest. To point out he was an adult and allowed to drink as much as he wanted to if he did it safely (he was ignoring his current risk of drowning off the dock). He wanted to argue like he was a lawyer before the courts, but his tongue was silent as he looked at her expression. Those beautiful doe-brown eyes of hers were reading him again, and he didn't want to know what assessment she was able to make of him at this time. He didn't suppose it was very flattering.

From the back of his mind, words and sentences began to form. Words he never wanted to speak, ideas which he had thought anchored with concrete shoes in the deepest depths of his mind. They were freed and wanted to be heard.

"Margaret," George began.

"No," she replied sharply, darting up like an escaping rabbit.

He blinked. Life was harder to understand when other people were in it, which is why he could successfully understand everything without the waters muddied by the presence of others. It reminded him why he was always better off alone.

He looked up, surprised to see she was still there.

"Whatever you're about to say, you're not going to say it until tomorrow. I don't care if it's what I'm hoping to hear or dreading to hear, you need to say it sober. You can't use a bottle of champagne as an excuse for what you say, I won't let you."

She cast the bottle into the lake, where it landed with a splash to punctuate her words. "Good night," she said, and turning on her heel, she walked back to the house.

The sound of Margaret's departing footsteps left a wake in George's mind, just as easily as the boats crossing through the lake had that day. Unsettled, he was stuck in a net of thoughts he was desperately trying to untangle. The words which had almost come to the surface—were they better left here on the dock and forgotten?

CHAPTER 19

In Norse mythology, Loki, the trickster god of mischief, was chained in the bowels of the earth to a slab of rock where a poisonous snake's venom dripped onto his head. George never thought he would find that particular myth relatable, but he certainly did right now. His head throbbed in such a way he had never known possible. Through the pounding of dwarves against his skull, George heard a voice telling him this was a bad idea, he should get in the car and drive away. There was no reason he needed to see Margaret ever again; surely he could successfully avoid her until the day he died. Despite the protestations, the reactions, and the nausea, he knew he didn't want that. Taking a deep breath, he knocked at Margaret's door.

After what seemed like a lifetime, she opened it. There was a cheerier attitude than he expected.

"Yes?" she asked, then observed, "You're dry now."

"I am. Would you mind taking a walk around the lake with me?"

She nodded. "Give me a minute."

Three minutes later, she opened the door again looking far more put together than George would have expected for taking three minutes.

The two walked to the lake in silence, and began walking down the path adjacent to the lake which crossed through every yard of every home on the lake.

"Hungover?" Margaret finally asked.

"When it's this aggressive, I call it a 'pullover.' Gravity alone isn't causing me this much pain."

Silence fell again.

Finally, George stopped. Margaret stopped. He stood, looked at her, and opened his mouth to speak, but no words issued out. Normally, it didn't matter the context or condition, he could talk about anything. There were only three times in his life George had ever found himself speechless; this made a fourth. Swallowing, he tried to speak again, forcing air out in an incoherent "Ahhhh."

"Are you okay?" Margaret asked, her face balancing between amusement and concern.

He took a deep breath. Last night, with the champagne, all the words seemed so easy to utter. They were there waiting to be unleashed. Now he found himself fishing for anything that resembled the words he wanted and needed to say. Open mouthed, he looked like a fish drowning on dry land, gasping for oxygen. His head throbbed, the venom dripping against his mind as surely as it dripped against Loki's face. Forcing his thoughts to stop panicking, he looked at Margaret, her eyes, nose, and smile. It reminded him of his first word, and he said it as proudly as if it was the first he had ever spoken.

"Irrational."

"Pardon?"

"That's how I feel. It's even irrational I feel at all. When I see you, talk with you, the very fact I want to be around you and like you is irrational and ridiculous."

Margaret pursed her lips; the direction of the conversation was not as she had expected. "You like me?" she asked.

"It's irrational!" George repeated, waving his hands in the air and pacing back and forth. "We've only known each other a short time. I've insulted and belittled you, abandoned you, used you… There's no rational reason you would ever want to be around me or like me. I am an unpleasant person at the best of times. *You* are not unpleasant. You are a kind-hearted woman who's willing to listen, to be generous to someone as arrogantly decided as myself. Even Paulo is a nicer man than me."

Margaret snickered at this. "Paulo is nicer," she agreed, "but he's also as decided as a kaleidoscope and reminds me of a stone in your shoe you can't seem to shake out."

"I shouldn't care," George went on, his pacing speeding up, "There is so much to lose by talking with you, but I am. Everything inside me is screaming to launch into the lake, steal a boat and get away from you as fast and as far as possible. You are a danger to my cultivated freedoms. It is all so… so…"

"Irrational," Margaret answered, smiling. "But you don't always need to be rational."

She leaned in and kissed him. The flush of passion was like flint and steel striking, lighting a small flame of feeling within each of them.

An audible cough interrupted them. A group of middle-aged women were waiting for them to clear the way so they could continue their walk. Reluctantly, the couple parted. Smirks and congratulations were given by the women as they passed. George blushed like a tomato.

"Would it be fair to believe you share my feelings?" he asked, a hint of doubt still edging his voice.

"No," she replied, "I don't find it nearly as irrational as you do. I think it's quite reasonable that I like you and you like me."

They continued walking around the lake. The morning was still early, and only a few eager fishermen had made their way out onto the water. As enjoyable as the heat of the moment was, George didn't waste time before thinking to the next step.

"Given the context of where we are and who we're with, I'd rather keep things a little quiet," he admitted.

"It's not like we're engaged," Margaret said. "We don't need to tell anyone anything. For now, we can just get to know each other without everyone else... interfering."

Interfering, that was a good word to describe it. He might have used the word 'meddling.' Between his mother and Helen, he could only imagine what misery would come on him during the rest of this trip if they discovered what had happened. This was why private lives were best left private.

"It's decided, then."

"Yes," she agreed, "but I do expect you to take me out for coffee."

"Certainly. Which won't seem weird. After all, we're friends."

"Yes, friends. Do I get to read your book now?"

"After enough time has passed to make sure this wasn't an elaborate plan to get to read it," he said with a grin.

She laughed aloud, and gave him a smile as warm as the rising sun.

They made it back to the Newcastle home in time for breakfast. The aromas of bacon and pancakes drifted from the kitchen to the patio as George and Margaret came up the steps. Before they could enter, George stopped Margaret. "Important question before we go any further," he said seriously. "Pancakes or waffles?"

"Pancakes, of course," she said with an "are you kidding me?" expression.

"Brilliant, just making sure," he replied, "And one more thing before we go inside." He looked around once to make sure no one was looking and, cupping her face in his hands, leaned in and kissed her.

She smiled. "Let's get some breakfast."

The company was all up and about in the kitchen, Mrs. Austen giving Henry Newcastle an extra hand collecting the pancakes as he flipped them off the griddle. Samantha making sure the bacon didn't burn. Paulo and Charles keeping Chelsea company at the kitchen table. Helen watching everything around her from her perch on a stool by the counter. The scene was so domestic, you wouldn't imagine there were dozens more guests asleep in their rooms or an ice sculpture melting in the backyard from the night before.

"Good morning," Helen said, seeing the two enter. "Early walk?"

"Ran into Margaret as I was taking a short walk around the lake," George said quickly. He wasn't worried people would enquire further; the reality is, people are easily consumed with their own interests, rarely summoning the energy to look outside of themselves.

"Breakfast is ready!" Henry Newcastle declared, removing the checked apron he had been wearing to avoid griddle splash.

Everyone found a seat at the table—everyone except Helen, who remained on her stool by the counter, and Margaret when she decided to join her there. George found himself sitting next to Chelsea, and tried not to notice the ice in her eyes when she looked at him.

"Nearly done with your draft, George?" Mrs. Austen asked.

"An excellent question," Henry Newcastle added with a smirk.

"I'm not certain which of you cares more, my mother or my editor," George replied with a laugh. "There's a readable draft which will be ready for submission by the end of the week. Honestly, I'm waiting to send it until we're done so Henry doesn't feel the need to look at it while I'm in the same building as him."

"Probably a smart choice," Henry conceded. "After all, we're on vacation. We should enjoy it. Plenty of good food, a beautiful lake, and friends."

At the word 'friends,' George and Margaret's eyes darted to each other and darted away.

It seemed a smart choice to keep the conversation off of himself, George reasoned. When the spotlight focuses on someone, they don't question who's operating the light. "What do you and Charles have planned today?" George asked Samantha.

Before Samantha could answer, Helen interrupted. "What do you have planned today, George?"

"Nothing at the moment," he replied, glancing at Helen and trying not to scowl.

"That's hardly characteristic," she prodded. "You're usually the man with every plan imaginable. Chelsea, do you have any suggestions?"

George couldn't decide whether Helen was being annoying, bitter about his attitude last night, or just herself.

"A long walk off a short pier?" Chelsea ventured, her voice pleasant but edged.

He could hear Margaret stifle a laugh, but didn't look her direction.

"It would be an excellent day for swimming," Mrs. Austen agreed. "The beach, sand, and sunshine. Everything you could want in a summer vacation."

George had no intention of wasting his day at the beach, shaking sand out of everything at the end of the day, his senses assaulted by people on the beach dressing for the bodies they wanted instead of the bodies they had.

"The beach sounds like a great idea," Margaret piped in, sipping her orange juice.

The beach wasn't such a bad idea, George reflected. After all, he could read there just as well as anywhere else.

CHAPTER 20

Seagulls by the lake. Even apart from the seeming wrongness of the name, they were a nuisance. Who needed rats when you had gulls? Aside from their constant presence and constant poop, they made constant noise. Squawking in unison to ensure you didn't ignore them. George, however, was immune to their cries. If you could ignore the most annoying of people, you could ignore the most annoying of wildfowl.

"George Austen!" Paulo called, testing the correlation.

George's eyes never shifted from the page in front of him. He was reclined on his beach towel in the same position he was in when he arrived fifteen minutes ago. He left for the beach at the precise time to arrive as planned, he would leave the beach at the precise time planned to return. This was the virtue of driving your own car.

"George Austen!" Paulo repeated, voice hurried, needy.

Carefully, George evaluated mentally whether this was a more hurried and needy tone than Paulo usually expressed. Against his better judgement, his eyes rose beyond the page to see Paulo carrying several beach bags his direction. Despite his close proximity to the ground, it didn't appear Paulo's balance was very good. As amusing as the idea of Paulo tipping like an egg would be to watch, George got up to help. After all, the last thing he wanted was the lemonade to spill.

"Thank you, George!" Paulo said with relief when he had unloaded two bags to George's shoulders. For a man whose blood appeared suited for the warmer climate, he was perspiring enough to water a garden.

"Which bag is the lemonade in?" George asked, glancing casually through the bags contents.

"I don't think we brought any," Paulo answered, still gasping for breath.

Well, now there was absolutely no point to being here, George thought.

"Hi," Margaret said, passing by the pair of baggage mules. Of course, George might have other reasons to be there.

"The beach is glorious today!" Mrs. Austen announced with delight, clasping her hands together. She had grown up visiting the beach, if George recalled correctly. A distant grandparent had been interested in boats, which lead to lots of time on the water or near it. It was a joy their mother had shared with her children, even if they didn't appreciate it nearly as much as she did.

Everyone settled like a camp of hobos around where George had already stretched out his beach blanket for reading. He resumed his relaxed position and reached for his book. It wasn't heavy reading; if it fell from a boat, it was more likely to float than sink. A paperback thriller from the forties someone had had the good sense to republish.

He was about to open his paperback to the page he had marked, when Margaret had set up her claim next to him on the right. Momentarily distracted, he couldn't help but notice she was wearing a very attractive swimsuit that revealed much more of her than he had seen before.

"A picture would last longer," she said with an ironical smile.

"It wouldn't do justice to the real thing," he quipped just loud enough for her to hear.

"Race me to the pier?" Helen asked Margaret.

Without answering Margaret started off towards the water. Helen immediately sprinted to catch up.

Free to resume his reading, George rolled back to the ideal position for just the right amount of sunshine to illuminate the page without blinding him.

To his left, Chelsea stretched out her beach towel and began sunbathing. She was wearing the same bikini she had been when they were boating and swimming. Their eyes briefly met and she gave him an unpleasant look he tried to ignore.

"Son?" Mrs. Austen said, indicating he should join her.

Dutifully, he replaced his bookmark and joined his mother. "Yes?"

"Did you and Chelsea have a tiff?" she asked quietly.

"Something like that."

"Fix it soon," she insisted. "No sense in you two spending the rest of the weekend giving each other the cold shoulder."

It wouldn't make a difference for the rest of his weekend, unless Chelsea decided it was worth escalating from dirty looks to dirty deeds. Saying this to his mother might be a fruitless endeavor, so instead he nodded and thanked her for the advice and returned to his book. Advancing past the first murder to the investigation of said murder. Just as the hero found his girlfriend lying in a pool of blood in his office, he was interrupted by a feminine voice saying, "So, whatcha reading?"

It was Margaret's voice. Which, George decided, meant he should probably not ignore it. He looked beyond the page of his book and met her dark brown eyes.

"A mystery novel," he replied, and returned to his page.

Margaret cleared her throat. George looked up from the book again. "Are you enjoying the beach?" he asked politely.

"Not as much as I could," she admitted.

"How could it improve?" he asked, trying not to sound impatient.

"You like mysteries. Perhaps you can solve this one?" she suggested with a smile.

George gave it a moment's thought, and believed he had the answer. Reaching into his bag, he extracted... another book.

"Here you go," he said, tossing her another murder mystery he had brought as a backup.

She smiled sweetly. "This isn't quite what I had in mind."

George was already back in his book, reading a well-written description of how blood-stained furniture was harder to resell.

Rolling her eyes, Margaret stretched out next to George with the book he had offered her. She decided to give it a few pages before returning it to him with a snide comment about how she didn't want to get tan lines in the shape of a rectangle on her face, even if he did. Surprisingly, she became more invested in the story of the hard-boiled detective pursuing justice than she expected. Still, it didn't stop her from dropping it by Chapter Four to provoke George to action again.

"Are you planning on swimming at all today?" she asked.

George looked up from his book, at Margaret, then at the water. "Why would I?" he asked, and returned to his book.

Margaret was beginning to appreciate why Chelsea had pushed him into the water twice this week already. Sighing, she flipped onto her back and looked up at the big blue sky, where only a few lazy clouds were crawling by.

"When did you learn to read people?" George asked, looking up from his book. It was a question that had simmered at the back of his mind, with never an appropriate opportunity to ask.

"Always?" she ventured. "It's a lazy answer, but mostly true. I've always been adept at intuitively knowing."

"Which makes you a devil at playing poker?" He chuckled.

"We should try a game, you can find out for yourself," she teased.

"How do you think it carries into your writing?" George asked. "If at all."

Margaret thought about the question a moment. "I probably see characters more realistically. I can describe their emotions through their expressions and actions more accurately because that's how I see and feel them in others. You're an abstract thinker, how did you ever take to the creative trade of writing?"

"You mean how did a cold-hearted intellectual start writing fiction?" he amended with a smile. "I've always been a storyteller, even if the stories are more of a mental exercise than anything. Creating conversations with people I'd never met or didn't speak to was a habit as a child which became what I do today."

The revelation held a flicker of an image to Margaret's mind of a quiet boy with few friends who retreated to ideas instead of people. An unstated loneliness he'd never admit to. Byronic perhaps, but also a petri dish for unrepentant self-interest.

"Do I dare ask about your family?" George asked, interrupting her thoughts.

"You know the Newcastles already, they are about as close to family as I have. The misfortunes of being orphaned as an adult."

"I'm sorry for asking so carelessly."

She shrugged. "You didn't know, and I don't talk about it."

He accepted her unspoken request to change the subject and began what became a long conversation about books and literature. They bantered and debated the merits of their favorite authors with the rest of their friends around them fading away as their conversation narrowed the world to only themselves. It wasn't until everyone else had packed their things and were kicking sand at them they realized it was time to leave.

Dinner was an uncomfortable recreation of that day's breakfast. The balance of the guest book had been emptied during their beach trip, with a collection of birthday cards and notes left behind for Henry to proofread at his leisure.

George had Chelsea to his right and a perfect eyeline to where Margaret and Helen were seated at the breakfast bar. He was tempted to try grabbing hold of the conversational frame and moving it as he wanted, but after how today went, it just wasn't in him. It would require more energy than it was worth. He was done, spent, ready to go home, ready to get back to his own coffee shop, ready to get back to his study.

He and Margaret hadn't talked much since the beach. Slipping away to Boxed and Burlap had been his plan, but it had been foiled by an overeager mother. No, the only person he could blame for his plans slipping away was himself. He could bear the irritation and wouldn't foist it upon anyone else. Margaret, for her part, seemed more amused at it than anything else. George reflected on a quote he had once read: "Life is a comedy to those who think and a tragedy to those who feel." Better to laugh and think, he decided. Better still to keep his trap shut.

"George, what do you think?" Helen asked.

"I think a lot of things," he replied quickly, returning to the present, "but have no idea what you're asking me about."

"Morning activity gets the rest of the day off on the right foot or not," she explained. "Samantha doesn't think it makes much of a difference."

"Morning activity can be essential," George said, confused that this was even a question.

"Are morning walks usually a part of the routine you subscribe to?" Helen asked, an eyebrow raised. Now he knew where she was going, he glanced at Margaret to see if she had caught the same wind yet. Helen noted the glance, and her face entertained a smile of complete delight. She didn't shout her conclusion, or self-congratulate in front of everyone. Instead, she looked at George and asked, "Are you two going to start dating?"

"Chelsea and George have gone on several dates," Mrs. Austen supplied ignorantly and happily.

"George and I aren't dating," Chelsea said. "She's asking about him and Margaret."

As George's face turned enough hues of red to become a paint swatch, Margaret answered Helen. "We're still figuring it out."

"You don't even like Margaret," Mrs. Austen said tactlessly.

"I think you should talk to George about this privately," Henry Newcastle advised her with a gentle pat on the hand.

"What about Chelsea?" Mrs. Austen continued.

For her part, Chelsea didn't turn any shade of red, but calmly explained to Mrs. Austen she and her son were never dating, and, nice though he might be, he wouldn't make a very good husband for her. George was grateful she left out the part about suggesting they jump in the sack and pushing him into the lake. He didn't see his mother reacting well to that part of the story.

Excusing himself, George rose and walked outside through the sliding door to the patio.

The sun hadn't set yet, but it was visibly declining. Like watching the British Empire after the First World War—still proud, but the height of its glory behind it. George took a deep breath, inhaling the sweet smell of the lake like he had when he first arrived at the lake not long ago. It helped. It drew out the nerves that he was surprised to find attacking him so violently.

"Hey," Margaret said, walking up beside him. "Want some water?" She was offering him an icy glass.

His hand trembled as he took it and drained the liquid from between the ice cubes. "Thanks," George muttered, looking at his trembling hand with disgust. "I thought we'd at least get to figure out what 'us' meant before everyone else could try to," he complained.

"If you'd like, I could save us some trouble and open up a dictionary, or a thesaurus if you'd like, for some other variations on 'us,'" she offered.

"As much as I like doing things by the book, I think we could be a little more creative than that," he admitted, giving her a smile.

Taking his hand, she laced her fingers through his. It was a quiet assurance, but it was enough. Looking into her eyes, he knew a dictionary wouldn't be needed. Although, it was tempting.

CHAPTER 21

S itting in his usual chair at his usual coffee shop, George was at rest with the world. The discord and dissonance which accompanied relocation from his natural environment dissipated, and the energy he had expended in a long weekend of surprises was beginning to recoup. Satisfied, he drank his coffee with a small smile.

The first draft of *Until All Graces* was sent off to Henry Newcastle. It had allowed him to wrestle with romance on an intellectual plane, where he could understand and articulate it. Which was a good thing, since now he was fighting to articulate it in a real context.

Things between him and Margaret were clear for the moment. They agreed not to rush into anything, but wanted to explore what future they might have. Usually, George knew in an instant what he wanted, what he believed the future too look like. Here, he was less certain, more shy to declare anything more than he'd already said. Admitting to liking her was one of the greatest struggles he'd faced in years; to do something about it was another obstacle he saw looming in his future.

It was decided he'd visit her in Des Moines later that week. Then they could have dinner and get to know each other more without the eyes of everyone else watching them. It was good, it gave him time to contemplate, to reason, to evaluate the risk. Margaret was a variable to his life that he hadn't accounted for, a variable he had decided to exclude long ago.

Arguing against his reservations, George reminded himself he had enjoyed each moment he spent with her over the weekend. Having her there made him forget about the things he could have been doing otherwise. Just remembering her smile made him feel warmer inside than any cup of coffee or single-malt scotch ever had.

"If your smile got any more satisfied, I'd be worried there was a canary in there," Anthony Stapleton said, taking the seat opposite George.

"You look like you need some coffee," George observed, noting the dark circles under Anthony's eyes.

"I do, I desperately do," Anthony agreed, taking a deep breath. "But, Katherine wants us to remove caffeine from our diet."

"So, order decaf coffee."

"Katherine doesn't see it as that simple," Anthony replied, wringing his hands like an addict going through withdrawal.

"So you came to the coffee shop to... *smell* the coffee?"

"At least it's something. I can drink it vicariously through you."

"You could always order tea instead," George pointed out.

Anthony gave him a glare, communicating in no uncertain terms he wouldn't be replacing coffee with tea anytime soon.

"Anything interesting happen the rest of the weekend?" Anthony asked with assumed nonchalance. He tried to keep his features serious, but broke into an impish smile.

"Who told you?" George asked wryly.

"You're the one who's always calling me a spy." Anthony shrugged. "I have my sources."

"Samantha."

"Samantha," he admitted. "But she wasn't clear on all the details, so amuse an old married man and tell me about it."

Starting with the moment the Stapletons left, George explained how things had gone with Chelsea, then Margaret, and how he and Margaret had admitted to a growing affection for one another.

After digesting the story, Anthony gave his friend a broad grin and pat on the shoulder, saying, "You've had quite a vacation. I would have given up coffee to see you squirm like that."

"You already did, and you did it for nothing," George reminded him.

"Point, but I have a happy wife whose smiling face I get to go home to tonight."

"Point, but you still don't have any coffee."

"Where's your book at anyway, the one Margaret pushed you to write in the first place?"

"I chose to write a romance on my own," George said defensively. "And it's been submitted to my editor."

"Now you get to decide on your next project while trying to woo the heart of a fair maiden."

"I'm not certain she's very fair," George said sarcastically. "Rather biased, actually."

"Everyone's biased, especially to you, Mr. Rationality," Anthony replied. "Don't hold her biases against her, or you'll find yourself asking where it went wrong sooner rather than later."

"You're saying I'm going to mess this up?"

"Not necessarily, but at least from my experience, I've asked where I went wrong a half dozen times already, and I'm married."

"You and I are different people."

"Which means you'll make your own mistakes."

George shrugged. He rarely made mistakes. Reason guarded him against them.

"Don't be an arrogant ass," Anthony pressed, reading his friend's thoughts. "That's the first mistake you might make, when you assume you won't make any. It's easy to think you can do no wrong when there are no consequences to what you do. If you want to make things work with Margaret it means consequences, good and bad."

George crossed his arms and tightened his jaw. "It's a little insulting when everyone is so condescending. Yes, I know there are consequences. They are what I'm evaluating."

"Evaluating?"

"Opportunity cost," George replied, drinking his coffee.

Anthony sighed. "Just explain, it'll be easier that way."

Stepping onto his metaphorical soapbox, George explained the opportunity cost to pursuing a relationship. Time spent trying to woo Margaret was time not spent writing, or doing countless other things that offered a more certain outcome.

Listening, Anthony nodded patiently. When George finished, he said, "I think you're overthinking this."

"Everyone else under-thinks," George retorted.

"Yes, there's a cost and a risk. It's like poker, you have to ante up to play the hand. You might win, and you might bust, but you have to play to get the answer."

"I could fold," George observed.

"Haven't you folded enough already?" Anthony challenged. "I don't mean to sound condescending, I'm just trying to prevent..." His voice trailed away.

"You want to prevent history from repeating itself," George finished irritably. Anthony nodded. "It won't," George assured him. "I refuse to let that happen."

The way he said it didn't fill Anthony with much confidence. He remembered when George had said he refused to let that happen in the past, in almost the exact same seat. It was a time he didn't like to remember.

It was always a little aggravating, and more, when people were trying to be nice—or, even worse, helpful. Perhaps it was this above all else that had George reluctant to share about his interest in Margaret with anyone. Anthony was not the only one to offer patronizing advice. Sitting in his library, working on his morning pages regardless of novel, George was interrupted by Samantha entering without a knock.

"Yes?" he asked.

She was beaming with excitement. "I like Margaret."

"Brilliant. So do I," he replied, and returned to his pages.

"Which is why I want to make sure you don't ruin it."

"The faith in your big brother is overwhelming," George said, dripping sarcasm. "Doesn't anyone believe in me?"

"You believe in yourself, and that's why I wanted to talk to you," she replied smartly. "Margaret's a nice girl, and you are... well, you. And you can be a little much in many ways, and I'd rather you didn't scare her off by acting like a bigger ass than you are."

"I'd argue I'm just as much an ass as I appear and then some, and she's seen it."

"Look," she said, taking a seat across from his desk, "you can't pull the 'I'm a jerk' card every time you do something insensitive or idiotic. Putting it in terms you might understand easier, she's going to expect a character arc where you stop doing stuff like that."

"If you're done dispensing the unnecessary advice, I've got work to do."

After giving him a cocked eyebrow and large sigh, Samantha rose from her chair and went to the door. "I should have remembered that part about casting pearls before swine," she declared dramatically.

"Thank you, Samantha!" George said loudly, as she made her exit.

George typed a few more words in his morning pages, the ones he had known he needed to type when she entered, but then stopped. It was annoying to have these extra voices, but though he discounted them aloud, he couldn't entirely discount them inside. He knew well enough how disregarding what people said entirely was a fault. It was why he still occasionally read what critics said about his books. On an impulse, he reached for his phone and sent Margaret a text of little meaning or substance. A smile danced across his face when she replied with something equally forgettable and unimportant.

An email from Henry Newcastle greeted George the following morning. It asked if he could drop in on Friday to talk about the first draft of *Until All Graces*. It was surprising; Henry must have heard George was coming to Des Moines to see Margaret and was taking the opportunity to meet in person rather than discuss the inevitable thoughts on tweaking the first draft. It was rare George ever sent in a first draft. More often, he waited until the completed manuscript was ready. Because both Henry and the publisher were skittish about his attempt at a romance novel, they had asked (just short of demanded) for an initial draft when it was completed. Why worry about it? George thought. Just sit back and let the comments come. He knew he could polish it to gleam in the eyes of every critic at every outlet.

Without a second thought, he replied to Henry that Friday would work perfectly fine. As a side benefit, now he had a good chance to surprise Margaret by coming to town early.

CHAPTER 22

Samantha had hoped George would simply notice. He'd see the wide smile, the radiant glow, the joy bursting from within her heart, or at least the diamond ring on her finger. Her brother noticed none of these clues, and instead was wrapped up in whatever world he carried within him.

It was Friday morning, and they were sitting across from one another for breakfast. He was packed and ready to leave for Des Moines, and classically oblivious to his surroundings. For a man who put up such a stink over his precious home being rearranged, he could go days without actually paying attention to any of his surroundings. She was tempted to make a game of it, see how long it would take before George noticed the cues to her engagement, but she didn't have the chance. Their mother surprised them by showing up for breakfast, and she certainly noticed things like diamond rings.

"Samantha!" Mrs. Austen exclaimed with every kind of happiness. She hugged her daughter close and immediately began peppering her with questions. "How did he propose? When did it happen? Was he on one knee?"

Puzzled, George looked up from his breakfast and bacon. Within the space of seconds, he went from pleasantly enjoying coffee and consideration to having his serenity shattered by his mother's violent squeals of delight. To answer his confusion, Samantha managed to extract her hand from her mother's embrace to wave her engagement ring for George to see clearly.

His eyes widened with understanding as the diamond glittered in the morning light. Looking down at what remained of his breakfast, he discovered his appetite had vanished, replaced by a sinking weight he couldn't quite describe.

"No," he said. The words were instant and cold.

Quiet as he had spoken, the sentence dropped like a chandelier striking the floor. Mrs. Austen and Samantha parted. Turning, the sister looked at her brother and asked, "What did you say?"

"No," he repeated. It wasn't framed as an entreaty. It wasn't a request. It was spoken like an edict of a king to his kingdom, or a master to his slave.

Knitting her brows, Samantha steeled herself for an argument that she hoped wouldn't be made. Mrs. Austen began to speak, but she cut her off. "Mother, I need to talk with George alone," she insisted firmly.

Looking from one child to the next, Mrs. Austen wished she could settle this for them but saw only the iron will of each ready to strike the other into submission. Reluctantly, she walked to the door. "Congratulations again," she said to Samantha. "Safe trip," she said to George and retreated from the house.

The two siblings stared at one another, unflinching gazes that said as much as their words would. George's eyes were as blue as ice and just as cold; so were Samantha's. Though not known for her hardness, she was just as capable as her brother of expressing her displeasure with a violent glance.

"I forbid it," George declared, breaking the silence. "Charles isn't good enough for you."

"This isn't your decision," Samantha said. "It has nothing to do with Charles and you know it. We're in love and we're getting married, with or without your blessing."

Rapping his fingers on the table, George looked out the window. Turning back to his sister he said, "It isn't in your best interest."

"My best interest?" she repeated with a laugh. "You mean it isn't in *your* best interest. Come on, admit it, you don't want me to go because it makes things inconvenient for you."

He clenched his jaw and fumed without response.

"For the past five years, I've lived to make your life easy and possible. I've solved your problems, over and over again. Now, I want to live my own life."

"I never asked."

"You never asked, you simply expected. You never even asked what happened to Isabelle at the party."

"I assumed you handled it."

"I did, and now you're horrified at the prospect of having to handle things yourself. You haven't had to live beyond your books and the page in front of you. When I leave, you actually have to start."

"I lived before you, and I'll live after," he snarled back.

"Everyone asks why you are the way you are. Why you're a calloused, heartless bastard. And I defend you. I tell them they don't know you, and it's just your rough edges, but the truth is they're right. You only care about yourself and your self-interest."

Without saying another word, George rose from his seat. Walking to the closet, he picked out his overcoat. Giving Samantha one last glare, he shut the door behind him.

Letting out a long sigh ending in a sob, Samantha drooped like a wilting flower. Tears sprang to her eyes, tinged with bitterness and betrayal.

CHAPTER 23

The entire morning was spent driving and fuming. Trying to ignore his annoyance, George listened to classic rock music until he arrived at the Newcastle home a little after noon.

George marveled at the decision Henry had made to move from the Chicago suburbs to Des Moines, Iowa of all places. He speculated it was make himself just that much harder to reach or drop in on without warning. Growing up as a token member of the Newcastle family, George recalled the days when they lived nearby and the house was filled with authors and creatives of all kinds at all hours. It was the perfect place for him to get a taste of what authors celebrated and feared, their joys and sorrows. A little salon where he was exposed to great ideas. Occasionally he considered trying the same open door policy himself, but he knew he was the personality to occasionally join, not host himself. He was mostly right, but failed to take into account the death of the late Mrs. Newcastle in changing the domestic life of his mentor. It was this which had triggered the Newcastles to make the lateral move westward and retreat from being accessible to everyone at any time. From Des Moines, Henry could go where he needed. His home was his, no longer a hostel for the creatives of the Midwest to congregate. Earlier in his career it had been a useful way to meet the up-and-coming authors and established masters. Now, it would probably require more effort than it was worth if he were to try it again.

Parking the car, George took in a deep breath. He knew if he walked in with the frustration of his conversation with Samantha, it wouldn't be fair to Henry, or to his book. He was a professional, and professionals managed their emotions. Resolved, and forcing a good humor, he stepped out and strode for the door.

After his knock, the door opened and George was greeted by Helen's unsmiling face.

"Hello Mr. Austen," she said with disinterest.

"Ms. Newcastle," he replied with a nod.

"Daddy's in the study. He's expecting you."

"Doesn't everyone?" he replied, forcing a smile.

"I never do," she reposted.

"That's why I'm winning," he whispered.

"Don't get ahead of yourself, you've still got plenty of feet to fall," Helen cautioned, leading him to the study.

Almost everything in the study was familiar to George. In many ways it was like his own study, but much cleaner and better organized. Bookcases covering every wall; to the right, the shelves were filled with books Henry used for his own reference, and to the left, books that Henry had shepherded through production and publishing. Each copy signed by the author he had worked with, a memory and an investment for the future. An oak desk stood like an island in the center of the room, drawing the attention of anyone who entered to its power and the person who sat behind it. It was only when George recognized the other visitor he was surprised—as was she.

"Hi George!" Margaret said. Leaping up, her expression was confused, but she gave him a kiss.

"It's good to see you," he said, with a warm smile.

"George, please take a seat," Henry offered, indicating the other chair.

Sitting down, George glanced at Margaret as if to ask if she knew why she was there. Her look only asked him the same question.

"I've read your draft of *Until All Graces*," Henry began, "and it's good, but..." He hesitated, then sighed. This wasn't a conversation he wanted to have, but he had a solution. "The book has promise, but I'm afraid it's not quite what we were hoping for."

"It's an early draft," George replied. "It can be tweaked."

"Yes, well, I think I have an idea about that."

It began to dawn on George the reason Margaret had been invited to this meeting, and his assumptions were confirmed when Henry explained his idea.

"*Good Intentions* has performed incredibly, and Margaret's name is being talked about. We think the best option here would be to have Margaret become the co-author of *Until All Graces* and do a pass over what's currently written and collaborate to finish it. It gives Margaret another credit quickly, and gets this book finished so you can move onto the next one. As far as I can see, it's a win-win all around."

George's jaw tightened instinctively. The calm he had been forcing through sheer willpower after his argument with Samantha was fading. Whatever clarity he had managed was evaporating. Yes, the book was incomplete, but it was a first draft. He still could polish it into something. There was no need for an extra person meddling with his story. As a writer he was the god of the pages, and Henry had just asked him to surrender his complete divine sovereignty.

"I love it!" Margaret declared enthusiastically, looking at George with a warm smile.

"Considering your relationship, I thought it might work," Henry admitted. "Who better than a writing couple to finish this?"

George still didn't say anything. The presumption of a still undefined relationship as an excuse galled him.

If Henry noticed George's silent rage, he wasn't planning on calling attention to it. Instead, he continued breezily, "Let me know how you both want to work out the details. Have your agents come up with a reasonable breakdown for each of you in royalties, credit, and the like. They might as well work for their money."

He proceeded to give his thoughts on the draft as it stood, and Margaret listened attentively, jotting down thoughts in a notebook she had extracted. For his part, George remained silent. He had been around long enough to know Henry would email him a complete list of thoughts and suggestions. He saw no point in wasting ink.

In brief, the basic issues were undeveloped minor characters who were going nowhere, in a couple of places the female protagonist was portrayed contradictorily, and other continuity errors. The editor shared his expectation Margaret would bring her thoughts on the story after reviewing it herself. She nodded excitedly. George had been reluctant to share what he had written; now she'd actually get to play in his sandbox.

When Henry had finished, he indicated he had another meeting in a few minutes, but was delighted to have both young authors working on this and expected great things. George wanted to hang back a moment to speak with Henry privately about what he was proposing, but Margaret pulled him away with her.

As they left the home, they had a few words with Helen. Learning of the proposal as Margaret excitedly shared it, she smiled, looking at George and intuiting the conflict which was already forming inside him.

"Sounds like a brilliant idea," Helen agreed. "I'm sure Margaret's going to offer some insights to what you were trying to write, George." It was her use of the word *trying* which twisted the knife ever so delicately, and she knew it. In response George gave her a mustered smile which was flawless in execution, if not sincerity.

"What are you doing here so early?" Margaret asked George when they were walking to their cars. "I didn't expect you until tomorrow."

"It was supposed to be a surprise," he explained. "It seemed like a good idea at the time."

"And a great one now," she agreed, smiling.

Before they went to dinner, Margaret insisted on taking him to her local coffee shop. Arriving at Smokey Row, George was impressed by the atmosphere. It was a lot like a classic soda fountain and a bar mixed together, though a little more crowded and bustling than he preferred. After ordering, and waiting near the bar to pick up his coffee, he decided that, as nice as it was, here was not a place where he could become a regular.

"Here's where I wrote the first part of *Good Intentions*," Margaret shared.

"Do you remember what you were drinking at the time?" George asked.

"I think it was an iced caramel macchiato. It's my typical order anyway."

They drank their coffees in silence, George was trying to decide quite how to properly react to the polite request Henry made to robbing him of *Until All Graces*. A decision made more challenging by how engaging Margaret was, even when she wasn't saying a word.

"What will your next book be about?" she suddenly asked.

"I don't know," George replied. "I haven't given it much thought. Henry wanted me to ghostwrite Senator G— after the party. I hope it's still an option. What about you, what will your next book be?"

Margaret paused a moment before replying, "It will be another romance, but I think this time it will be about a detective falling in love."

"Why a detective?"

"I think it would be interesting to see how someone who solves mysteries solves the question of love. It's not original, but as you've often noted, very little is. The differences are only found in the writing of the thing."

"Is there a mystery beyond the questions of love?"

"Probably, there are plenty of mysteries in the world. A detective could work on any one of them. Have a suggestion?"

"Organ harvesters would be the ironic answer," George replied with a smile, "but I've always thought the most romantic of mysteries are the ones which include vast sums of money."

"A heist?"

"The theft of a priceless object is much like love, isn't it? Plenty of parallels you can use to distract or enchant the readers."

Margaret liked the idea and could see the doors it opened—more importantly, the windows it opened for a master thief to slide into the story. Admittedly, the idea of the thief falling in love with the detective was a little tried, but already she had an idea which could breathe life into it. A female detective and a polished gentleman thief: a duo that could chase each other across continents. It just might work. Quickly, she sketched out the premise to George, who nodded his approval.

"The tagline could be: 'The first heart he couldn't steal,'" he suggested.

"Are you a writer or something?" Margaret asked with a laugh.

"Frequently I'm something," he quipped.

"I think this is why we'll make good collaborators," Margaret decided. "I can't wait to dig into *Until All Graces* and add my touch to it. You haven't told me much, but based on reading your other books, I'm guessing the women will need a little rounding in their characters."

George cleared his throat. "*If* we collaborate, you mean."

Margaret's eyes shot up from her coffee. The draft of her changes to the novel slipped out of her mind as she evaluated what George had said. "What do you mean *if*?" she asked. "Henry said..."

"Henry said," George interrupted, "but I still haven't. It's my book, and I still haven't decided if I want to have a collaborator on it."

"What's to decide? It's a great opportunity for us to work together."

"It's my story." George shrugged. "I'm struggling to see why there's any legitimate reason to have you involved."

"I see. Chelsea can help you with your book but I can't?"

"Chelsea—"

"Helped you write your book, but you don't want *my* help. I'm just an author of a successful romance novel, and she's a floozy. Clearly she is the more helpful."

"That's unfair," George defended himself. "Yes, you've written a successful novel, but this is *my* book. You're judging Chelsea as unfairly as Henry is judging my first draft. If he let me review it a couple more times, he never would have thought about involving you in it." Here's where he should have stopped, where he should have paused to notice Margaret's reactions. There's a difference between the blush of a maiden's cheek and the flush of anger rushing to the face of a woman scorned. Instead, George added, "The only reason he even suggests this is because he thinks we have a relationship."

Margaret had it; the final sentence was the final straw. Raising her voice, she said, "George Austen, you are a self-consumed, self-conceited know-it-all. This was a fun idea that you immediately decided against because it might infringe on your ego! You didn't really even consider it, did you? Come on, answer me."

"No," George replied without hesitation, his jaw tight and his eyes cold.

"I thought you had changed, but that was my mistake," Margaret said bitterly. "You're the same person who left me in that chapel, and the same person who insulted someone's writing without remorse."

"I am who I am, and it sounds like you had the wrong impression about what you were getting into," he said icily.

"What I see is, you don't want to take a risk or put yourself in a position where you might not be perfectly put together. You're probably not even scared about involving me in the book, you're scared about involving me in your life. Eventually you have to deal with real stuff, either with me or anyone else."

"I've always been real," he retorted. "This *is* real life, Margaret, not scribbles on a page! There's no sense in deluding ourselves. We can't live in your fictionalized world. This is reality, and I'm the one who's choosing being real."

Looking him up and down, Margaret searched for some hint of heart, but found none. She had hoped he would fight for her, but the fight he had wasn't to win her. His eyes were all ice and resolution, glinting with a cold hardness that she had only seen in flashes but now steadily radiated from his entire body. His mind was made up, and so was hers. In one final explosion of anger, of vengeful rage at how George had pulled on her heart only to throw her away the moment he felt threatened, Margaret rose from her seat and poured her ice water over his crotch.

"Goodbye, George," she said, dropping the plastic cup on the floor and storming out."

CHAPTER 24

The slamming door woke Samantha with a shock. Hurrying on her robe, she stuck her head through the door to see George storm into the house like a thunderclap. His expression was as grim as she'd ever seen it. When he caught her gaze, he growled and stalked away to the study without a word, the vestige of his scowl floating behind him.

The next day was tense. George didn't leave his study, and Samantha could only guess why he was home sooner than she'd expected. It was clear things hadn't gone well in Des Moines, but that didn't matter to her anymore. She was done fixing her brother's problems. It did, however, pose awkwardness for her move. After their blowup, she decided it was best she move back in with her mother until she found a place of her own, if that was even needed depending on when the wedding would be. It didn't take long to get her things packed and moved. Settling back into her childhood room, she briefly wondered how long it would take George to notice she was even gone.

Whatever suspicions Samantha harbored were confirmed when Mrs. Austen returned from a visit with her son. Apparently after two days of silence from the dark cavern of his study, the mother decided it was time to investigate. It was never a good sign if George was laconic, and after two hours prying single-word sentences from her son, she learned precisely what had happened between him and Margaret.

"It's fine," he muttered, enveloped in his armchair with a tumbler of whiskey at nine in the morning.

"Have you spoken to Samantha?" Mrs. Austen asked delicately.

He scowled in response and tipped back his whiskey.

The maternal instinct made Mrs. Austen want to step in, to drag her children in front of her and insist they make up and apologize. George principally was in the wrong, but Samantha ignoring him wouldn't make things any better. She was painfully aware any action on her part would be met with stiff resistance from each of them; it would take careful cajoling to ease them into some kind of settled peace. It needed to at least happen in time for Samantha's wedding so they wouldn't have incomplete family photos.

"You were wrong," she chided George.

"Hmpf," he mumbled without conviction. "Which time?"

"Both times, dear, both times."

He swirled his whiskey in the glass.

"Drinking isn't going to help," she counseled.

"It isn't going to hurt," he countered, taking another long sip.

Knitting her brow, Mrs. Austen reached out, seized the glass from him, and poured the remaining contents into a ficus plant struggling for survival.

"I don't think the green thing is going to appreciate the twelve-hundred-dollar single-malt scotch you gave it," George observed dryly.

"Wallow about your book, wallow about Margaret. That's your choice. You do not get to leave things with Samantha like this. She's your sister, and you will make things right," she ordered. The declaration made, Mrs. Austen rose and left George to glower from his armchair in solitude.

It had been a week since Samantha had moved out, barely longer since she had been proposed to. In that time, she hadn't said a word to George. He hadn't made any attempt to repair things, and she wasn't about to lift a finger to change the dynamic. She still felt the sting of his words, and the imperious way he believed he could destine her fate was intolerable. But, a part of her ached at the idea of him callously cutting ties without a second thought. He was her brother, after all. Angry as she was, she still loved him.

Now, however, was not the time for Samantha to ruminate on her brother or his clear absence of humanity. Tonight was about Charles. It was the annual North Shore Chiropractor's Association Benefit Gala. They were raising funds for spinal curvatures and bent backs of children with a silent auction. Charles had been the one to put the night together, and while the glamour fell short of the birthday of Henry Newcastle, it still promised to be a festive night.

It the preceding weeks, Samantha had been a sounding board for the various ideas and opportunities Charles had been considering to make it a special night. In a particular flight of fancy, he had asked, "Would George consider saying a few words and kicking in a signed first edition of something for the auction?"

"Probably not," she'd replied. Even before the engagement and disaster in Des Moines, Samantha knew it would be far fetched. It was simple math: George didn't like Charles and wouldn't be inclined to do anything that might remotely inconvenience him for his sake. An evening spent in a room of Charleses talking about underprivileged children would be the kind of thing he'd sooner visit the South Side of Chicago to avoid. If there wasn't an angle for him to play, he wouldn't come to the game.

"How do you think the night is going?" Charles asked, taking a seat next to his fiancé. Lifting her hand, he gave it a small kiss.

Samantha giggled slightly, still giddy about the new ring on her finger. "It's a great night," she replied. "Everyone looks like they're having a great time."

"You have just as much to do with it as me," he said graciously.

Samantha smiled. She was good at arranging details and making sure everything was in the right place. It was what she'd done for years for George. Tonight, looking around at the party in completion, she knew what it was like to do it for herself.

"I know things have been strained at home," he said.

She stopped him by putting her hand on his. "Let's not talk about that tonight."

Charles gave her a small smirk. "What I was going to say, if you'd let me finish, is I have a surprise for you."

Cocking an eyebrow, Samantha said, "You think you can?"

"Oh, we'll see." He mused, patting her hand. "I need to settle everyone in their seats for the presentation tonight."

Once he ascended to the dais, Charles asked everyone to be seated and complimented the staff on doing a great job setting the evening up. A shower of applause drifted through the room. "I'd also like to thank someone very special to me—my fiancé, Samantha Austen, without whom none of this would be as grand as it is."

The applause sounded louder and Samantha gave everyone looking at her a polite nod.

"A special thanks to everyone who came out here tonight in the faith our surprise guest would be someone you'd like to hear, although most of you probably came for the bar regardless..."

Giggles from the crowd.

"Without further ado, our guest tonight is a New York Times best-selling novelist known for political intrigue and social commentary: George Austen!"

Samantha's head jerked when she heard her brother's name and saw him stride on stage and shake Charles's hand.

Taking the microphone, George thanked Charles for the kind introduction. He shared about how he had benefited greatly from chiropractic care as a child and was honored to be there tonight to pay it forward in the cause that brought them there together that night.

Shocked as she was to see her brother, what surprised her more was realizing this wasn't a canned speech. Over the past several years, she had seen him give talks like this multiple times, each one a script that was adjusted to the crowd and the cause he was there to address. This one was wholly original for tonight.

"I'd like to finish by proposing a toast," he announced, "to Charles and my sister Samantha, and their happy engagement. May it lead to many joyful moments to come."

The crowd toasted, and howled as it ended with Charles giving Samantha an affectionate kiss.

With the presentation over, George wandered to the family's table and sat next to Samantha and gave her a wan smile.

"I can't believe you convinced him to come," Samantha said to Charles.

"Actually," Charles admitted, "George offered."

She looked at her brother, giving him a tearful smile.

"I've missed you," he said quietly. Before he could say more, she interrupted him with a hug.

CHAPTER 25

Autumn

With resolution between the siblings, Samantha started dropping by the condo again to see how George was doing. It was unsurprising to see the place reverting to its condition when she'd first moved in. Books and papers drifting out from the confines of the study to everywhere else in the place. It was as if nature was beginning to reclaim a decayed and abandoned city, except instead of vines, trees, and shrubs the place was slowly being consumed by books and their byproducts.

She'd tried to suggest he hire a maid or cleaning service, but George ignored her. He was listless in their conversations. Distracted, he insisted, by how *Until All Graces* had stalled. He had called his agent, Frank, to work out things with Henry, but nothing was happening.

Anytime he was challenged as to why he was sleeping late, missing the gym, and spending more time at the coffee shop drinking coffee than attempting to write, the book was George's excuse.

Samantha suggested they go to the book store, to which George stared blankly and declined. Anthony suggested they book an African safari, a trip George had been trying to push for years.

George only said, "Maybe later." Mrs. Austen proposed setting up another date with Isabelle, to which George didn't even say anything, only grunted on his way out the door to the coffee shop.

No matter what was put in front of him, George was disinterested. To the average person, he was as human as anyone, but to those who knew him well he was a completely different person. The drive, the push, the heightened character he added to life was gone. For the present he was only a cardboard cutout of himself. In image and appearance you wouldn't suspect a thing, but the moment you looked for the energy or story he usually brought, it was apparent he wasn't the same.

"What should we do?" Samantha asked.

Congregated around the kitchen island, Samantha, Mrs. Austen, Anthony, and Katherine were assembled to manage the crisis.

"I don't see why we should do anything," Katherine said. "He's been easier to talk to lately, maybe we should just let things be."

"He didn't want to go to Egypt. Egypt! He's been trying to convince me to go see the pyramids with him for years!" Anthony said.

"Which is hilarious, considering he hates the beach," Katherine added unhelpfully.

"There's got to be a way to pull him out of this funk," Samantha said. "We're the people who know him best, we should be able to do this. I caught him reading a copy of *Good Intentions* yesterday, and based on his reaction you would have thought I found him with a copy of *Playboy*."

"Obvious question, but has anyone tried to reach Margaret?" Anthony asked.

"I tried. She only spoke for a few minutes and basically said it wasn't her problem, and really it's not," Samantha said.

"He says it's just about the book. Maybe it's just that," Katherine argued.

"Ordinarily, I'd say yes, but he's never cared this much about writing something," Anthony explained. "The only time he's been like this was, well... the last time something like this happened."

"How long did it take for him to pull out then?" Katherine asked.

"Two years and a best seller," Samantha groaned, dropping her head in her hands. There had to be a solution.

"Have you considered..." Mrs. Austen began, but Samantha had already finished the thought in her own mind. Sighing, she reluctantly agreed it seemed like the best way to resolve things one way or another.

"I can call," Mrs. Austen offered.

"No," Samantha insisted, "I'll fix it."

All it took was one phone call, a call she had hoped to never make. Helen Newcastle had been suggested to call, but Helen couldn't do anything to help. She was too much like George, too self-possessed and self-interested. Samantha knew there was only one person who might speak sense to George right now. Dialing the number felt like she was making a deal with the devil, but it wasn't the devil who answered the phone. It was the original sin of George Austen.

CHAPTER 26

Ordering another wasn't a good option. It really wasn't. Sitting there, alone, he knew ordering another drink wasn't the right choice. He could feel the effects of the several previous orders coursing through his veins, affecting his perception of the world. That was what he had wanted after all, wasn't it? To change his perception.

His head hung down as the thoughts, memories, unbidden returned to haunt him anew. It still hurt, no matter how much he drank, how much he tried to stay distracted. Everything in his life had been about control, about reason and doing the smart thing. She was not the smart thing. Her influence distracted him from the religion of reason he had followed.

It ended as it was destined to end, the end he knew the moment his grasp was lost on the situation. That's what lead him here now, lead to him make the choices he had before, and the choices he would make going forward. Yes, another wasn't a good option, but it was the one he was going to take.

"Decaf, please," he asked the barista. There was already no way he was getting any sleep tonight, and not just because of the volume of caffeine he had already consumed. Still, there was no reason to force a heart attack where it wasn't needed.

When reasoning how to react, he chose the coffee shop instead of the bar. Drinking alcohol numbs, but it doesn't really offer viable solutions. Coffee, however, as a stimulant might give him the chance to think through or out of his misery quicker.

"We don't have a legal limit on how much coffee we can serve you, but I'm pretty sure you've passed the quantity recommended by some kind of Harvard study," Josiah said, passing George another espresso.

"Your commentary is noted," George replied, taking the coffee. "I'll probably only order ten or twelve more."

Josiah chuckled and walked away as George drank another espresso through chattering teeth. He had no doubt—whatever else might occasionally occur to him—it was his book that had brought on the crisis of the moment. He needed to get out of this slump and back to the state of standard of productivity to which he was accustomed. He needed to start writing again and needed to something to kick-start it, and the last time he drank too much alcohol it didn't go the way he had planned. Coffee just might be the thing to push him to the point he needed to get back to.

When the doorbell rang, George didn't think anything of it beyond its being another bit of stimulus entering his overactive mind. He was focused on his espresso and the results he hoped to find from it. When a red-haired girl took the seat across from him, it took a breath to register it was her, even with the accelerated pace of his mind.

"How you doing, George?" she asked, her voice as golden as it was the very first time he heard it, only now it wasn't accompanied by the singing of sirens.

"Hello Cynthia," he said coolly.

If you were to ask George, "Who hurt you?" he probably wouldn't answer. Only shrug it off with a sarcastic comment. The embodied answer sat across from him: Cynthia Brown. Red curls, freckles, prominent front teeth, and bohemian tastes in her style and appearance. Time had done little to change her; she was everything he remembered her to be.

"What have you been up to?" he asked.

"Recently a few of my paintings have been shown in local galleries, sold some too. I may dress like an artist, but it doesn't mean I want to starve like one."

"I saw some of them at the Armour Gallery when they did their last showing. Impressive to see how your style has developed."

"Thanks, and I read *Lord Wilmore*. Classic George Austen through and through. I was just glad a redhead didn't get murdered in this one," she replied with a dry chuckle.

"Authorial license is a marvelous thing," George admitted. "I actually had a draft where a redhead overdosed, but ended up cutting it."

"At least you were willing to add some variety to my ritualistic death." She laughed.

They were silent a moment, neither venturing a word. Uncomfortably each evaluated how the other had changed since they had last seen each other those many years ago. Had time softened or hardened? Seeing someone from the past provokes you to not only audit them, but yourself too.

"Of all the coffee shops in all the towns in all the world, you walk into mine. This isn't a coincidence," George observed.

"You're right, Bogart-Holmes. Just as dramatic as you ever were, too, but I guess some things can't be expected to change no matter how much time passes."

"We could banter for hours until we start arguing, so let's just get to it. Why are you here?"

"It always amazes me how your sister is such a sweet gal and you're such a tool," Cynthia replied. "She's worried about you, thought talking to me might make some kind of difference."

"You don't look particularly bothered," he observed, sipping his espresso.

"I don't really care," she replied. "In fact, if you never write again, I don't have to endure reading about another redheaded woman being butchered into thirty-seven pieces. Although, if rumor tells me right, maybe the next victim will be a brunette," she speculated, touching forefinger to lip in thought.

"My publisher rejected my novel," George vented, "and that stings more than it hurts. Cyn, I haven't had to worry about getting something published in years. They admitted it was good even, they just didn't want to take the risk it wouldn't sell the way they wanted."

Cynthia nodded, curls bobbing around her face. "Do I need to go to the counter to order, or is the squirt going to come and ask for it?"

"You order at the counter." George sighed.

"When I get back, we're going to talk about what's really bothering you," she warned, getting up and walking over to Josiah.

George's espresso was almost gone. He could probably bolt for the door without much trouble, but she'd catch up with him. Cyn always catches up with you, he reflected. Helen and he were thinkers and intellectuals; they could view the world dispassionately and disinterestedly. If either of them were to find the person they were speaking with vanish, they'd shrug and settle down to the silence. Not Cynthia. She was as creative as he was, but far more aggressive. She would follow him out the door and knock him in the back of the skull with a rock if needed. Relentlessness and ruthlessness were the very qualities about her that had first attracted him.

Coffee in hand, she took back her seat. As if she rode his mental train of thought to its last stop, she said, "Almost didn't think I'd see you when I came back. Made sure to get enough caffeine to hunt you down if I needed to."

"The book is what's really bothering me," George defended himself. "Maybe this is just the beginning of the end of my marketability as a writer."

"You know that's horse hockey. You're just coming up with a reason you can justify feeling bad for, instead of talking about what actually is making you feel like life is over."

George grit his teeth and clenched his fist. He could see why his family had called Cynthia, why she was the one asking these questions instead of one of them. She was a blunt instrument and not going to skirt around what she thought. She was willing to make him as uncomfortable as needed.

"You agreed to come here just to watch me squirm, didn't you?"

"Aren't you the one who always uses that JP Morgan quote, something about how people do things for two reasons, the right one and the real one? I think it applies here." She smiled. "I can both enjoy watching you writhe and do your sister a solid, I think it's the best of both worlds. So spill."

George spilled. He told her about how he and Margaret met, how they argued, how he admitted he liked her, how they broke up over his book, how she poured ice water on his crotch (she laughed at that).

"You liked her, you had chemistry, you even were both writers. You're telling me the reason you dumped her was because you didn't want to write with her?"

"You're simplifying it."

"No, no, I'm summarizing," she corrected. "You wanted her, had her… Here's what's confusing me though. When you were after me, you were willing to burn the world to ground. Yes, flattering, and also yes, creepy. Why didn't you do the same for Margaret?"

George didn't reply. He scratched his chin with the edge of his thumb and ruminated. "When I was chasing you, I couldn't see a reason you wouldn't be interested, I couldn't see a reason why it wouldn't work. With Margaret, I didn't have the luxury of self-deceit. This time I just knew better."

"As much as I'd love to take credit for your emotional scarring, you're the only one to blame there. Do you like flowers? Forget it, dumb comparison to use with you. Let's see... a well-made dinner. Is it any less good because you eat it and it's gone? Just because something's temporary, or won't last like solid granite, doesn't mean it isn't worth enjoying while it's here. You know this, you've probably got some snooty quote about it."

"'Cities and thrones and powers stand in time's eye, almost as long as flowers which daily die.' Kipling."

"Yeah. So, my point. Let's call it what it is—you acted like a massive jerk, probably because your ego was threatened. Massive mistake. Margaret sounds like a great gal, and hey, I loved *Good Intentions*, way more than your books. No redheads were murdered in it. Based on what you've done, there's probably a less than 3 percent chance she ever wants to hear from you again, so you should probably just stop moping and get back to whatever it is you consider living."

"What if..." George began. "What if I wanted to see if there was a chance?"

Cynthia laughed. "Then you have precisely the self-confidence you should have had before you dumped her like two-week-old chili."

"I think I've got an idea."

"If you hold onto it, maybe you'll find a few more," she quipped.

In the way that two old friends become reacquainted, they shared more banter and life history before she said goodbye. Each promised they wouldn't wait so long before reconnecting, each knew they probably wouldn't keep the promise. Their time as friends had passed; now they had different needs and different circles. George was encouraged to find the tug on his heart Cyn had once caused—she, his greatest temptation in the past—was gone. She was everything he remembered, but didn't hold him the way she had before. It was some small comfort out of all this. Her points were sound, even if he wanted to be deaf to them. He was left with a new choice to make.

George was about to leave when he heard Josiah call, "Mr. Austen, hold up!"

Taking his seat, George waited for the young barista to sit down across from him. "Yes, Josiah?" he queried, hoping the young man didn't need any more romantic advice. He doubted there was much he could confidently offer today.

"I just wanted to say thank you for the advice, it really meant a lot. It also helped a lot," Josiah said awkwardly.

"You're welcome. Dare I ask how it went?" George said, just as awkwardly.

Josiah sighed. "I asked Cassandra out to dinner tonight and she said yes, but I think she'll end up saying she just likes me as a friend. If that's the case, I'll be fine," he said with a shrug.

"You had the courage to ask, which can be hard, but the courage to accept you might not get the answer you want is harder still," George acknowledged. "Let me know how it goes, Josiah."

The barista nodded. "Thank you again, sir, have a great evening."

"Enjoy your dinner," George encouraged him.

It warmed his heart to know, in some small way, he had helped this boy. Perhaps, his advice would even help himself.

CHAPTER 27

Soon George found himself back in his study, phone in hand, staring at his call history. Three times he had called Margaret and failed to reach her. The first time he didn't leave a message, the second time he almost left a message, and the third time he left a message saying he was an idiot and wanted to talk when she had a chance. He was debating the merits of sending a text message when he heard a knock at the door.

"Yes?" he called.

Samantha let herself in and took a seat across from him. "How was your coffee?" she asked, a small smirk rebelling against her control.

"The owners of the shop are adding a legal serving limit because of me."

"What was it like seeing her again?" she asked seriously, worry briefly flashing across her features. Her greatest concern was seeing Cyn again would hurt him more than it helped.

George sighed. "It was good. Relieving in some ways, actually."

"Good," Samantha decided. "You seem to have a little life back. What are you going to do with it?"

"Swing for the fences, I guess. I've tried calling Margaret, she's not answering."

"She's got every reason not to. You were a prick."

"Thanks for the clarification, I was worried she was taking a shower," he replied sarcastically.

"This is a case of consequences," she reminded him.

"I'm sorry, you're right." He ran his hand through his hair in exasperation.

"And that is precisely what you'll say to Margaret when you see her."

"*If* I see her."

"*When* you see her. I've seen the way she looked at you, and that doesn't disappear over the course of a couple of weeks. If someone as cold as you doesn't get over it very quickly..."

Letting out a sigh, George leaned back in his chair and rubbed his face. "I'm the creator of my worst problems."

"We all are," she assured him. "It's part of being human."

"A restriction I haven't managed to overcome."

"People wouldn't care about what you wrote if you couldn't add care to it. Whatever is said about you being heartless, everything you've written proves the opposite."

"You're saying I shouldn't give up just because she didn't answer?"

"Wait until she pours boiling oil on you instead of ice water. That's when you know it's really over," Samantha advised, rising from her seat.

As she was about to leave the room, George halted her, saying, "Thanks for calling Cynthia. It helped."

She smiled. "No trouble, dear. I'm glad to see you've got your head back."

Instead of calling Margaret again, or sending a text message, George did the thing he should have started with: He called Helen.

"I was wondering when you were going to call," Helen said smugly. She had made him wait several rings before picking up. George could imagine the look of self-satisfaction on her face watching his name appear on her phone as it vibrated for her attention.

"I messed up," he started.

"Yes, you did," she affirmed. "Now you'd like to repent of your foolishness?"

"Yeah, but Margaret's not answering."

"Can't blame her, you were a prick."

"Yeah, I'd like to apologize for that."

"And you expect me to…"

"Help me."

The line was silent. If there had been a cord to the phone, George knew she'd have been twirling it in her fingers. She was doing precisely what he would have if the roles were reversed: looking for the angle and opportunity.

"What's in it for me?" she asked, drawing out the question with relish.

"What do you want?" he asked, shrugging.

She told him. Helen was specific about what she wanted, and how he would get it to her. What she would do in return was guarantee he would see Margaret. From there, it was up to him to not make the same stupid mistakes he had before. He tried to protest, to bargain for something else, but her mind was made up. She wanted it to hurt, and twisted the knife to make sure it did. They hung up after agreeing to the time and place on Sunday. George didn't doubt Helen would do everything she promised; at the price she was charging, she better.

"*Alea iacta est*," George said aloud. The die was cast, and now he had to wait to see where it landed. He pulled out a white legal pad from his desk drawer and unscrewed his fountain pen. Until Sunday, he had time to put his words to paper, to script his thoughts as best he could. Maybe this time he wouldn't be caught speechless or grasping for words. It was time to lean into the one strength he had, the one thing he had proven he knew how to do: write.

CHAPTER 28

In exchange for her yet to be determined price, Helen gave George a time and address, for which he was already running fifteen minutes behind. It came as some small surprise to find Chicago traffic could exist in Iowa. Bolting out of his car to make up for the lost time, George raced across the lot and to the door. Entering the directed building, he was greeted by a large sign reading, "Welcome Romance Writers of America Conference!"

Wherever she was, Helen must have been enjoying a good laugh at George's expense. He approached the registration desk, where one lone woman was scurrying back and forth behind the table hurriedly asking for names and shuffling them away or out the door. "Name?" she asked the now seventeen minutes late George.

"George Austen," he replied. "I might not be..."

After glancing at her computer the woman materialized a manila envelope and ID badge, nearly hurling them at him and indicating the door to get through. "Read what's in the envelope," she instructed. On the envelope it read, "Hall C."

Donning his badge, George entered the venue. He wasn't sure what he had expected to find, everything decorated in pink and hearts like Valentine's Day? Instead, it looked like every other writers conference he had ever attended, only with a significantly higher female demographic in attendance. He could spot a few men here and there, but not many. He could understand why, in general, most romance authors were women because those were the audience. Nine out of ten here, if they wrote anything, wrote the kind of fluff, near smut, that played on the idea of chiseled chests and heaving bosoms. Unbidden, George's nose began to wrinkle at the thought. He was of the opinion if you wrote sex, it should be classy at the least. Before he could continue drifting down the rabbit hole, he saw a large map of the place and was reminded he was already running late and didn't have time to meditate on the nuance of physical intimacy and the written word. Hurriedly, he started scanning the map looking for Hall C.

"You're George Austen!" a voice called.

"I am," he replied absently, "and I'm also running late."

"Isabelle, this is George Austen," the woman said, calling a friend.

To George's complete surprise, it was Isabelle Monroe, the first of his investigative dates and the one who had accosted him at the Newcastle party. They looked at one another with some shock.

"You," Isabelle said coldly.

"You're a designer, what are you doing here?" George asked with confusion.

"Sally here is a romance author and she invited me to join her."

"Oh, it's only two books," Sally tittered. "My latest, *The Highlander's Abs*, has been a best seller on Audible in adult reading."

Under other circumstances, there would be a dozen different sarcastic remarks George would have enjoyed making about "adult" reading, but he was in too much of a hurry to share any of them.

"Congratulations, I really should be going," he said, trying to escape to the stairs.

"Tell me about your romance, is it as novel as your others?" Sally asked suggestively.

This interaction was going nowhere, and neither was George if he couldn't find where Hall C was. Before he snapped, yelling out he didn't care about adult reading, Isabelle's annoyance, or the abs of Scottish barbarians, he was confronted with the sure thing to push him over the edge.

"George Austen!" Professor Paulo Castillo said, spreading his arms and grasping George in an unwanted embrace. "Such a pleasure."

"Paulo, I need to—"

"Yes, yes, we have much to discuss," the professor began. "I need to take you to Hall C. Excuse us, ladies," he apologized with a bow. "They were supposed to tell me when you arrived, I expected you a half hour ago," Paulo explained as they walked off. "Sorry for the mishap."

"You were expecting me?"

"Of course, my department is helping the conference host here. Helen explained everything, and I was happy to help. How could I not, after your generous offer? I cannot begin to describe how grateful I am. Your insights will be invaluable to completing my book.

When Helen said you had asked to read a draft and share your feed-back, I was beside myself with complete joy."

George's eyes widened, realizing the expense of Helen's help was his own suffering. Nothing more, nothing less, and nothing else. "It'll be my pleasure," he managed to say, as he and Paulo walked down the corridor to Hall C.

"Mine as well," Paulo agreed, beaming with delight. "Everything is arranged," he declared, opening the door of Hall C.

Immediately, George was greeted by a conference volunteer who asked, "Are you George Austen?"

"I am."

"We've been expecting you, let me take you to your seat."

"Good luck!" Paulo said, waving goodbye.

"I have a reserved seat?" George asked the volunteer and waving absently toward the closing door.

"Of course."

George was ushered to reserved seating near the front row. The room was nearly filled—far more so than he would have antic-ipated. The elaborate degree to which Helen had gone to put him in contact with Margaret was impressive, though self-indulgent. Reminding him she was every bit as clever and precise as he was himself. Looking around the room, George didn't see Margaret anywhere, but he had finally made it where he was supposed to, even if it was twenty minutes late. He had been so distracted, he actually didn't even know what this workshop was supposed to be. Based on the number of chairs in the front, it might even be a panel discussion. Maybe this was Helen's way of torturing him a little before he could meet up with Margaret? He hadn't even opened the manila envelope yet. As he was about to do so, the volunteer for the conference got to the microphone and began to introduce the speakers.

"On today's panel we've got a lot of great authors here. First, let's give a warm welcome to George Austen!"

More was said about George, his work, and his upcoming romance novel, but he didn't hear it. Instead, he quietly cursed Helen Newcastle as he left the envelope on his seat and made his way to the front of the room and took a seat in front of the microphone.

Other panelists took their seats as their names were called, each taking a spot. Finally the volunteer finished saying, "And moderating today's discussion is Margaret Clarke, best-selling author of *Good Intentions.*" Margaret appeared from the midst of the crowd and took the microphone from the volunteer with a round of applause.

Evaluating the situation, George realized he still didn't know what the panel was even about, and it was about to be moderated by a woman he had insulted and spurned. Panicking would do him no good. After all, he was a smart cookie. Listening to the other panelists talk, he would soon pick up on the thread of why they were there. In fact, Margaret might just ignore him altogether.

"I think everyone wants to hear from George Austen first," Margaret announced, a round of applause validating her choice.

Curses on Helen Newcastle and any children the harpy ever spawns, George thought. He had to think on his feet and wander into a sentence which he hoped wouldn't take him straight off a cliff. "Romance is a challenge, as much in fiction as in life," he began, receiving a welcome chuckle from the audience. Emboldened, he continued, "No matter what topic we're here to discuss, *there* is both the heart and soul of what we are gathered to celebrate and facilitate." A cheer from the audience, and George thanked the muses for giving him such a miraculous gift for bullshit. Glancing at Margaret out of the corner of his eye, he wondered if she had caught a whiff of what he was shoveling, but she didn't meet his gaze.

Smiling at the audience, she asked, "Mr. Austen, how does conflict relate to our topic today? I remember you've expressed a strong opinion about it before."

George had strong opinions about almost everything; this did nothing to narrow the field for topic. Quickly he replayed their conversations in his mind to try to pull anything of weight that they could be discussing. They had talked about writing often enough, it could be anything. Assuming an air of contemplation, he hoped to hide the confusion that was swelling beneath the facade. Nothing material came quickly enough to mind, so back to the manure pile he ran. "Conflict is the essence of story. Without it we have no plot, no excitement, no movement. Our topic is instrumental in conflicts; it directly pulls and pushes the train of plot forward and backward."

Listening to himself, George began to think he sounded a lot like Paulo—spewing a lot of words without any real substance to support them. Meaning of any fashion lost in the sea of similes and contradictions. Margaret looked at him blankly, apparently having expected something far more concrete than he had offered.

"I thought you believed 'what' was always more important than 'why'? It's a contrary opinion that would have been interesting to highlight," she said.

Face reddened, George was spared any further questions as the fellow panelists were asked questions that steadily revealed the topic of the panel. They were in fact discussing how 'why' drove their characters, how it was the principle element of any plot, and the slavish devotion that every writer should give it to create, define, and propel any narrative. George had definite opinions on this—opinions which he had fumbled the opportunity of sharing.

"Mr. Austen, I wanted to circle back on your thoughts as to the matter of 'why.'"

"'What's' the point," he stated dryly, to absolute silence from the crowd. Unperturbed, he continued. "No, genuinely, 'what' is the most important element of the plot, at least it is for me. 'Why' is motivation. 'What' is theme and action. 'Why' is subjective. 'What' is objective."

"You believe 'what' carries more weight than 'why'?" Margaret asked.

"Yes. We can judge actions, but not motivations. Motivations matter little except as the reason to propel a 'what,' a deed. What someone has done or not done says more about them than their motivations." Here George's voice changed from conversation to lecture, the didactic form of speaking he slipped into without much thought. "'What' is done. What we do matters more than what we say or profess, because actions matter more than words. In a book, it is the actions of the characters that move the plot along. Saying how they feel means nothing unless action is taken through the plot which they either agreed or disagreed with. Life is the same. The objective, the 'what,' makes the difference and pushes life forward and around more than any way. In romantic fiction, 'what' becomes the actions or lack thereof that moves characters toward or away from one another. If we spend all our time asking questions about why a character does this or that, we never get anywhere in the plot. Authors who make 'why' their only focus, without turning any attention to how it relates to 'what,' wander through their books struggling to commit to one thing or another." He spoke with confidence, with certainty.

"You've got a romance novel in the works, Mr. Austen. Do you care much about the 'why' of any of those characters?"

"Only to the degree it propels their 'what,'" George reiterated.

"You're more interested in the egg than the chicken that laid it," Margaret said with some bite. It was with patience she had listened to him, but the way he confidently declared what should be done, as if his method was the only right one, finally made her snap. "Actions can be judged, even if motivations can't. What if after declaring his affection and love, a male protagonist does nothing to try to keep his love interest around? You're saying the 'why' is irrelevant because their actions spoke volumes?" Margaret asked.

"I'm saying the 'why' is subjective," he insisted, worry seeping in about where the conversation was headed.

"Let's ask the audience if they can guess the 'why' from those actions. How about it?"

The crowd responded enthusiastically. It was beginning to become apparent, to both the other panelists and the audience watching, there was unexpressed hostility between George and Margaret. With the attention busybodies and gossips give to their craft, everyone gazed with curiosity to see if this conflict would actually erupt before them.

"What do you think is the 'why' of a man who wouldn't fight to keep a girl he claimed to like?" Margaret asked at large.

"He plays women, to manipulate them for his own sick amusement," one woman commented.

"He was only interested as long as he didn't see someone better," another mused.

"He realized she wasn't an easy girl."

"He wanted to break her heart."

"He didn't want to break his own heart."

"He didn't think she was worth it."

Margaret thanked the people who offered their thoughts, while George patiently squirmed and tried to keep his expression as neutral as possible.

"It could be any of those reasons, or none of them," Margaret decided. "Like Mr. Austen said, motivations are subjective until they are clearly written or explained. But actions speak; they are loud and clear as crystal. The fact remains what it is: He let her go without a fight, without even a protest to keep her around! Speculation abounds to why he would do something like that. 'What' is clear and 'why' remains ambiguous and unspoken. In this case at least, I can agree with you, Mr. Austen. The 'why' is almost immaterial, because the 'what' here is enough to supply any want of question." She fixed George with a glare that might have withered a lesser man, but he met her gaze without flinching.

"'What' establishes a character's actions," he retorted. "It follows the famous edict to show, don't tell. But in fiction we do tell. We rarely leave an action so ambiguous as to leave the reader unable to follow either the story or comprehend what's about to happen. In real life—"

"In real life," Margaret interrupted, "some of us tell, and others leave you in the dark not caring if anyone follows the narrative or not. Some of us actively subvert the story and challenge expectations simply because they can and they don't care!"

"Maybe they do care, maybe that's their 'why'!" George spat back.

"They have a terrible way of showing it!"

The volunteer who had started the panel and was standing in the corner nervously put up a hand to catch Margaret's attention.

"We've run out of time for the panel today," Margaret announced, calming her voice. "Any final comments or thoughts our panelists would like to share?"

The other panelists, sharing their first words in the past twenty minutes, gave their thanks to be there and encouragement to the audience for their work, both published and in progress. When it was George's turn, he simply said, "Be on the watch for *Until All Graces*, my first romance novel, co-written with Margaret Clarke."

A murmur passed through the room. This was the first they had heard there was a co-author, and it was Margaret Clarke, of all people. Many immediately decided the verbal attack was the overflow of authorial disagreements. For her part, Margaret was shocked and stared at George, mouth agape. It lasted for a moment. Then she dropped her microphone and ran off the stage and out of the room.

CHAPTER 29

D ecorum be damned. George didn't amble off the stage after the applause had finished, he leapt off the stage after Margaret, trying to catch up with her. He wasn't going to let his sense of propriety get in the way. She'd run away in the past, and he'd let her, but not this time. Besides, he had publicly committed to her being his co-author.

It was a gesture he had thought would be well received, perhaps would smooth things over. In no scenario had he anticipated chasing after Margaret through the hallways of the convention center.

"Margaret!" he called, but either she couldn't hear him or was ignoring him. He dearly hoped it was the former.

He followed her down the stairs and began to lose sight of her in the crowd. Admittedly, if she left the building he'd have a better chance of finding her, unless of course she got to her car... Speeding towards the doors, George almost missed her. Catching sight of her out of the corner of his eye, he skidded to a stop and rounded back. She was sitting on a couch near the exit. Slumped over, head in hands, sniffling back tears.

"Margaret?" George asked gently, sitting beside her.

She didn't reply.

Awkwardly, he said, "You know, I don't run. If I was being chased by a bear I'd play dead and hope it worked instead of stepping an inch."

"Bears would outrun you anyway," Margaret sniffed.

"Which is why I don't see any reason to start running anytime soon. Playing dead is usually a better strategy. But I didn't think that would work out so well onstage back there."

She laughed, then coughed. George offered her a handkerchief, and she stared at it a moment before taking it.

"Alright," Margaret decided, dabbing at her eyes and sniffling, "Whatever you're going to say, I'll listen, but no promises. If I decide to get up and leave, I never want to see your face again."

George took a breath, and exhaled slowly. Clasping his hands together, he steepled his index fingers and touched them to his lips. Usually here was where he would lose his words, but before he left home that morning, he had taken the initiative. He had to express feelings, emotion, push what was burning within him into sentences of meaning and fulfill the ultimate use of language: expression of the heart. Rather than leave this to luck or hope, he had written out what he wanted to say.

Tentatively, like a child taking its first steps, George began to speak, remembering what he had rehearsed. "You are incredible, and I apologize. I did nothing to keep you from leaving, I belittled anything you could contribute and discounted you as both a writer and as a potential partner. You matter. Your presence is like a muse by my side and your absence dragged me to Hades' doorstep. In the past, I thought Hades was as good a place to write as any, but even in paradise, I wouldn't be able to without you. Margaret... I love you."

Whatever the preamble, however many allusions and mythologies he used, Margaret only cared about those last three words. Three words for which battles have been waged, kingdoms won and lost, and countless words of bad poetry strung together. For those three words, men and women would go to the ends of the earth, and George had said them to her.

Surveying George, Margaret read his body. From the way his brow was furrowed, his eyes gazed at her, and his hands were clenched, down to the direction his feet pointed. She looked for even a glimmer of the reserve that he held to keep the world at bay, but it was gone. Not a stitch of armor remained. He was wholly and utterly vulnerable. If she wounded him, it wouldn't be a knick; it would be a mortal blow. He was within her power, and they both knew it. Her decision was made, and she was not cruel enough to prolong his suffering.

Hard faced, Margaret got up, sighed, and smoothed her skirt. "Well," she said, "are we going to get started on your book or not?"

George nearly leapt off the bench and took her in his arms, pulling her in for a deep kiss.

Watching the young couple kissing in a passionate embrace, someone began to clap. Others joined in as they became aware of the two lovers (this was the Romance Writers of America Conference, after all). George heard the applause out of the periphery of his senses, but it didn't matter. He was holding his muse. From now on, only her applause mattered.

EPILOGUE

A little over a year after the publication of *Until All Graces*, George Austen was on a well-deserved vacation. Sitting on the balcony of his hotel room, he sipped on espresso and picked up his newspaper. Procuring a Chicago paper wasn't the easiest thing in Cairo (the one in Egypt, not to be confused with Cairo, Illinois). It was an effort well worth his energies, knowing what was waiting within its pages.

Turning to the society column, he found the article he was looking for and began to read aloud. "It was an occasion to be remembered, treasured even. In attendance was Senator G—, the Chicago mayor, notable authors from across the country, and even American intelligence officers. Normally, a group of this kind is only assembled to discuss and speculate about national security. Today, they gathered to celebrate the wedding of George Austen and Margaret Clarke. Mr. Austen was dashing in the truest sense: tuxedo and tails, with a rakish smile and a glint in his eye defying the age-old tropes of the nervous groom. Everyone he spoke with noted the surety of his voice, ease of manner, and self-possession. The bride was radiant."

"Radiant?" Margaret called from the bedroom.

Joining George on the balcony in a terry cloth robe, she gracefully dropped on his lap. "You went to the trouble of writing the column about our wedding and used a dozen adjectives to describe yourself and *one* to describe me?"

"It was only a half dozen," George said defensively. "Radiant supplies all someone could wonder about you."

"Sure," Margaret said, rolling her eyes.

"If we read your column about the wedding in the Des Moines paper, it would probably be just as biased," George argued.

"Perhaps, but we'll never know since it isn't available online," Margaret said with a stretch and a yawn.

"My dear, if I can procure a Chicago paper in Cairo, don't you think I can also find a Des Moines paper?" he asked with a wink. Waving his hand, he revealed he had already done so. She reached for the paper, but George held it back. "Delightful reading, I'm sure," he said.

"We were there, we don't need to read it," Margaret insisted.

"I can't think of anything more pleasant to do at this moment than read the words you wrote, Mrs. Austen."

Getting hold of the paper, Margaret dropped it to the ground and clasped her hands behind George's head. Staring intently into his eyes, she said, "I've got a few alternative options to offer," and pulled him into a kiss.

The paper remained dejected where it had landed, as neither husband nor wife bent to retrieve it. Had he picked it up and read the article, George would have seen the title to Margaret's column: **"Romance is more than a genre."**

ACKNOWLEDGEMENTS

While not an awards speech, we'll see if I ever have that opportunity, this is the moment to thank and acknowledge those without whom this book you've read would still be a joke.

What started as a good humored, "what would a Jane Austen book look like from the man's side of the story?" developed into a real book through the help of the following people.

Thanks Mom, unlike Mrs. Austen you've given me both privacy and the space to write as I like. Thanks to my sisters, Maggie and Truth for indulging me in recitations of chapters to gain the female perspective on the story. A special thank you to my editor, Meghan Stoll, without whom my words would be less than they are now. Thanks Scott, for pushing me to finish a project, and for reading early drafts of a genre you don't actively choose to read. Thank you, Emmet, Maddie, and Grant, for reading early drafts and sharing your perspectives on the story.

Thank you to my friends who have contributed to this work in more ways than I could probably say. Even if unmentioned by name, your contribution to my story is indescribable.